P9-CDS-930

STALLION in SPOOKY HOLLOW

Ben M. Baglio

Illustrations by Ann Baum

Cover illustration by
Mary Ann Lasher

SCHOLASTIC INC.

New York Toronto London Auckland Sydney
Mexico City New Delhi Hong Kong Buenos Aires

Special thanks to Andrea Abbott

If you purchased this book without a cover, you should be aware that this book is stolen property. It was reported as "unsold and destroyed" to the publisher, and neither the author nor the publisher has received any payment for this "stripped book."

No part of this publication may be reproduced, stored in a retrieval system, or transmitted in any form or by any means, electronic, mechanical, photocopying, recording, or otherwise, without written permission of the publisher. For information regarding permission, write to Working Partners Limited, 1 Albion Place, London W6 0QT, United Kingdom.

ISBN-13: 978-0-439-02531-7
ISBN-10: 0-439-02531-1

Text copyright © 2007 by Working Partners Limited.
Created by Working Partners Limited, London W6 0QT.
Illustrations copyright © 2007 by Scholastic Inc.

All rights reserved. Published by Scholastic Inc., 557 Broadway, New York, NY 10012, by arrangement with Working Partners Limited. ANIMAL ARK is a trademark of Working Partners Limited. SCHOLASTIC, APPLE PAPERBACKS, and associated logos are trademarks and/or registered trademarks of Scholastic Inc.

12 11 10 9 8 7 6 5 4 3 2 1   7 8 9 10 11 12/0

Printed in the U.S.A.   40
First Scholastic printing, October 2007

One

"Look! We've reached the sea!"

Mandy pointed excitedly through the side window of the Land Rover as it crested a hill, and a broad, green sweep of land fell away to reveal the English Channel stretching to the horizon. The water was gray-blue in the late afternoon, with mist hovering above the surface like smoke as it heaved and rolled toward the shore. Mandy looked at the map on her lap. The grassy plain between her and the sea was Chaldon Down. There were no houses, and the only evidence of humans was a footpath along the cliffs. According to the map, it was called the *Jurassic Coast Footpath.*

The Jurassic Coast! What a fantastic name for such a wild, empty place. But this part of England wasn't known only for dinosaur fossils buried beneath its rugged coastline. This was smuggler country!

Mandy and her mom and dad had come to Dorset, one of the southern counties of England famous for smuggling in the eighteenth century. "Can't you just *see* smugglers riding across the Down on their horses or pulling goods over those cliffs?" Mandy said to her parents, with her nose still pressed to the window.

"Absolutely!" said her mom, braking as the Land Rover caught up with a slow-moving tractor. "Especially with the mist coming in and those black clouds building up on the horizon. These would have been ideal conditions for smugglers."

"The gloomier the better as far as they were concerned," said Mandy's dad, looking around at her from the front seat. "The best time to bring goods ashore was on dark, moonless nights with barely a star in the sky. . . ."

Mandy was amazed that anyone would risk being on the open sea in pitch-darkness. "How did they know where they were going?"

"They had helpers onshore lighting bonfires on the cliffs to guide them," said Dr. Emily Hope. "The same people would have helped them hide the smuggled silk, tea, or lace before the customs men could catch them."

"It sounds hectic," Mandy said, imagining smugglers frantically off-loading their cargo in the dark, with waves crashing all around them and customs officials patrolling the cliffs above.

"It wouldn't have been easy," Dr. Adam Hope agreed. "But there was good profit in it for the smugglers. There was a huge demand for the cloth and tea they brought in because ordinary people couldn't afford the high import taxes that the government had put on those items."

"What put a stop to it all?" Mandy asked.

"Smuggling hasn't ever really stopped," said Dr. Emily. "But it's a lot more sophisticated these days and doesn't involve basic things like tea and fabric. It's more likely to be counterfeit goods — DVDs, watches, things like that — or things that are banned, like certain plants." She stopped the Land Rover as a herd of Jersey cows began crossing the road just ahead.

A herdsman and his collie drove the cows from behind, and it was only when the last one stepped out onto the road that Mandy saw the sign on the roadside: WELCOME TO CHALDON HERRING.

"We're here!" she announced, peering ahead for her first glimpse of the place that would be their home for the next week.

The Hopes had driven to Dorset from their home in

Welford, Yorkshire, to spend the mid-semester autumn vacation in the village of Chaldon Herring. Both of Mandy's parents were veterinarians, and they'd agreed to look after the veterinary practice in Chaldon Herring for a friend, David Carhill, who was on vacation with his family in France. While the Hopes were in Dorset, they'd left their own practice, Animal Ark, in the care of a retired vet, Anna Sinclair, who lived about ten miles from the village. Dr. Emily steered carefully through the narrow village streets, past ancient stone cottages with sagging thatched roofs, a quaint church built of flinty stone, and an imposing manor house called The Grange, set back from the road. Dusk had settled like a dark gray blanket by the time they arrived at the veterinary clinic. In the Land Rover's headlights, Mandy saw two thatched, whitewashed cottages adjoining each other. They were set back from the road behind a tall wooden fence, backing onto Chaldon Down, which stretched all the way to the sea.

"It looks almost as nice as Animal Ark," Mandy declared.

They found the key where Mr. Carhill had said it would be — beneath a statue of a cat near the front door. "Trust a vet to have a garden cat instead of a garden gnome," Mandy joked. With its mischievous expression, the statue reminded her of her grandparents' kitten, Smoky.

Inside, an open wooden staircase led from the hall to the Carhills' spacious living quarters. At the top of the stairs was a huge open-plan living room and dining area with big overstuffed sofas surrounding a central fireplace. At one end of the room, a large double window looked out on to Chaldon Down. A bookshelf jam-packed with journals, thick books, and magazines spanned one wall. When Mandy took a closer look, she saw that most of the titles were about veterinary medicine or animals. "Plenty for us animal lovers to read!" she said approvingly.

There were other signs that animal people lived there: The doorstop was a bronze statue of an elephant, and a painting of a whale had the prized place above the fireplace. On the mantel, there was a framed photograph of a man, woman, and a smiling young girl with short dark curly hair. They were surrounded by geese, swans, and ducks.

"Are these the Carhills?" Mandy asked, for she hadn't met them herself.

"Yes, and it looks like they're at a bird sanctuary," said Dr. Adam. "That doesn't surprise me, because David's always been avian crazy!" Mandy knew that "avian" was the scientific name for all species of bird.

The focus on animals made her feel completely at home. And when she took her luggage to the pretty pink bedroom that was to be hers for the week, she was even more in her element. There were animal posters everywhere! Ponies, cats, dogs, bear cubs, even a wombat trotted, crawled, and lay cozily around the walls. It wasn't a room where a person would feel lonely for a minute. There was a note on the bed, addressed to Mandy.

Hi Mandy,

I hope you like my room. It's so cool of you all to take care of our clinic while we're in France. We'll be in the Camargue, where the wild horses and flamingos are. I can't wait to see them. Have a great time in Chaldon Herring.

Best wishes,
Heather Carhill

P.S. Happy Halloween!

Dr. Emily popped her head around the door. She smiled when she saw all the posters. "What makes me think this room belongs to another vet's daughter?" Mandy laughed.

There was one other room she wanted to see that night: the residential unit. Dr. Carhill had called before he left that morning to say there were five in-patients. The clinic nurse had kept an eye on them that day, but they needed to be checked again. While her mom and dad unpacked, Mandy went to find the unit. It was in a renovated outbuilding in the backyard. Inside, a note on the door of each cage gave details of the patients. There were two female Labradors that had been spayed, a bulldog recovering from an asthma attack, a black kitten who'd caught his foot in a mouse-trap, and a chinchilla with an ear infection.

Mandy freshened water bowls and bottles, changed soiled bedding, and then spent time with each animal, making sure they were all comfortable. The Labradors, Tumble and Tara, looked as if nothing had happened to them. They thumped their heavy tails against the sides of their cages and whined to be let out. "Sorry," said Mandy, patting Tumble through the wire, "the note says you can't go home until tomorrow afternoon."

The bulldog, Arnold, was asleep and snoring loudly. "At least you're snoring and not wheezing," Mandy said.

Both the kitten, whose name was Cocoa, and the chinchilla, Gem, were very shy. They peered out at Mandy from the back of their cages where they lay curled up in beds that looked like bulky doughnuts. "Maybe you'll trust me more tomorrow," she whispered.

Later, when she climbed into bed and closed her eyes, she thought she could hear the sea crashing against the cliffs on the far side of Chaldon Down. She imagined a heavily laden rowboat being tossed on the waves while a smuggler, dressed in black and wearing a broad-brimmed hat, pulled at the oars.

A knock at the door startled her. "Yes?" she said, switching on the bedside lamp.

Her dad came in. "I thought you'd like to read this." He handed her a dog-eared paperback book. "I found it in the reception area."

At first, the shabby paperback didn't look all that interesting. Then Mandy read the title and felt her heart beat faster. *Tales of Dorset Smugglers.* "It's *exactly* what I want to read. Thanks, Dad," she said, and turned to the first page.

The gale force wind tore at the roof. Driving rain pelted the window of Ruth's attic bedroom. She lay on her straw mattress, and pulled the rough woolen blanket tightly around her. She was trembling, not from cold but from fear. Fear for her beloved father, Robert Stickland. He should have been home by now.

Above the roaring gale, there came the sound of hoofbeats. Ruth leaped out of bed and ran to the window. Two horsemen were galloping up to the house. "Eliza! Wake up!" shouted one, jumping off his mount and hammering on the door.

Ruth heard the heavy bolt slide open and her mother's anxious voice: "What is it?"

"Robert's boat's gone down!" came the reply.

When Mandy awoke after a night full of stormy dreams, the paperback book was lying on the floor. She must have dropped it when she fell asleep reading the story of Robert Stickland. Apparently, giant waves had capsized his boat and he was never found. Ten-year-old Ruth and her mother, Eliza, had been left penniless, but the local villagers had taken care of them in return for all the tea and fine silks Robert had helped bring ashore.

After breakfast, Mandy and her parents explored the clinic before the patients started to arrive. Like Animal Ark, there were two treatment rooms, an operating theater, and a reception area with lots of chairs along the walls.

"I can't find the appointment book," said Dr. Adam, searching the desk.

"Maybe they have a different system," said Dr. Emily.

Mandy looked at the computer on the desk. It was humming so she knew it was switched on. She moved the mouse and the screen lit up. "It's probably on here," she said, looking at the desktop icons. She clicked on one that was labeled "SCHEDULE" and a spreadsheet of names, telephone numbers, and time slots appeared. Animal details and owners were in a file called "CLIENTS."

Mandy's dad looked over her shoulder. "Top of the line!" he said.

The first patient wasn't due for half an hour, so Mandy went to check on the animals in the residential unit. Outside, thick mist hung above the ground and she couldn't see much farther than the back fence. She started heading across the lawn, but a spine-tingling wail stopped her in her tracks. The haunting lament rang out again and then again, firing Mandy's imagination. Was it something to do with smugglers? Perhaps the ghost of a poor soul — Robert Stickland, even — lost at sea and doomed to cry out in misery for all eternity.

"Well, hello there!"

Mandy nearly jumped out of her skin.

"It's Mandy, isn't it?" The voice was bright and cheerful, the opposite of the eerie wail echoing through the mist.

Mandy turned around to see a young woman climbing

off a bicycle at the corner of the cottage. She was tall and willowy with long black hair held in a purple scrunchie.

"That's me."

"I'm Jessame Burrows, the receptionist and clinic nurse." She leaned her bike against the wall and unstrapped her backpack from the rack behind the seat.

"Hi, Miss Burrows," said Mandy.

Just then, a gorgeous dog raced around the corner and hurtled over to Mandy. It was about the size of a border collie and had a glossy brown-and-white coat.

"Hello to you, too, beautiful," Mandy said, kneeling down and patting the dog. "And what's your name?"

"She's called Impala. Pala for short," said Jessame. "And while we're on the subject of names, please call me Jessame. 'Miss Burrows' makes me sound like a schoolteacher!"

Mandy chuckled. "OK. Hi, Jessame."

Pala was wagging her stubby tail so fast it looked as if she might lose her balance. Mandy tried to figure out exactly what breed the dog was. Her long silky ears and soft, feathery coat suggested she was part cocker spaniel. "Cocker cross?" Mandy guessed, looking up at Jessame.

"Yep. Actually, a cocker spaniel and springer spaniel mix," said Jessame. "Also known as a sprocker."

"Of course!" Mandy said, realizing that while Pala had the beautiful domed head of a cocker spaniel, she had the height and brown-and-white coloring of a springer. She also had a dark chestnut-colored nose and marks like freckles on her muzzle. Mandy hadn't met many sprockers, but she knew they were sporting dogs, once used to chase down game. She knew, too, that they had a lovely temperament and were excellent tracking dogs.

"You know she's yours for the week, don't you?" said Jessame.

"She is?" Mandy said, delighted. "I thought she was yours."

"She belongs to the Carhills, actually," said Jessame. "Didn't David mention you'd be watching her?"

"He might have said something to my mom and dad," Mandy said. "But they were busy getting things together at Animal Ark before we left, so they probably forgot to mention it."

"It's been chaotic here, too," said Jessame. "And today will be no different. I'd better get on in there and start with the in-patients."

"I'll help you," Mandy said. "I was just going to see them, anyway." Across Chaldon Down, the ghostly wail continued. "By the way, what's that noise?"

"A foghorn," said Jessame. "Down at Lulworth Cove — a natural harbor with very steep cliffs. When it's misty, the siren warns ships about Man o' War Rocks. They're called that because they look like a warship, or 'man o' war,' when the tide is low enough to see them."

So the eerie sound had nothing to do with smugglers. Mandy felt a bit embarrassed. Good thing she hadn't said anything about ghosts. Obviously, Halloween was getting to her already!

After letting Pala into the house, Mandy and Jessame went to the residential unit. "This used to be a stable," Jessame explained, going inside.

While Jessame prepared the patients' food, Mandy cleaned out the cages. This was one of her regular duties at Animal Ark, so she felt even more at home than before. All three dogs were delighted to see her, especially Arnold the bulldog, who gave her a slobbery lick when she opened his cage.

The chinchilla and kitten were still shy, so Mandy didn't try to handle them. But as she put a bowl of fresh water in Cocoa's cage, she noticed that the wound on his paw was red and puffy. "That looks infected," she remarked.

"You're right, Mandy," said Jessame, coming over to take a look. "Let's take him in to see your mom."

Dr. Emily was still waiting for her first patient, so she was able to see Cocoa right away. "The infection must have set in overnight," she said, examining the paw. She prepared a shot of antibiotics. "We'll have to keep a close watch on this," she said, injecting the medication while Mandy held the kitten still.

"Mandy certainly knows a thing or two about veterinary work," Jessame said to Dr. Emily. "I might not have noticed that infection until much later."

Mandy's mom looked at her proudly. "She's a real vet in the making."

Mandy glowed with pride. She loved how her parents took her own ambition to be a vet so seriously.

"It seems you're well on your way already," Jessame said, smiling at Mandy. "If the Carhills knew, they probably wouldn't want to let you go home!"

After the morning patients, Mandy and her dad went shopping for groceries. The general store was in a small redbrick building squashed between two thatched houses. A tall, broad-shouldered man wearing silver-rimmed glasses was standing behind the counter.

"Ah! Adam and Mandy Hope. Good to see you," he greeted them.

"Uh, hi," Mandy said, puzzled that he knew exactly who they were.

Her dad clearly shared her surprise. "How do you know us?"

The shopkeeper smiled. "News travels fast in small

places. And David put a picture of you on the bulletin-board outside the village hall with a note to say you'd be standing in for him."

"Good idea," said Dr. Adam. He shook the man's hand. "Anyway, it's good to meet you, too, . . . uh . . ."

"Tony Farmer," said the grocer. He wore a knee-length blue apron with a drawing of a wagon and the words FARMER'S CHOICE on the front. He grinned. "Otherwise known as Tiny. David told me you were from Welford. Beautiful place."

"You know Welford?" Mandy asked.

"Very well," said Tony. "My wife comes from York. We go there every Christmas and always do a little touring of the area. Last year we had dinner in Welford, at the Fox and Goose."

Mandy beamed at her dad. It was their local inn!

"I thought the food was excellent," Tony continued. "Almost as good as the Gray Horse near Lulworth, just a couple of miles from here. You should give it a try." He picked up a pumpkin from a jumbled heap in one corner. "I bet you haven't had a chance to carve your jack-o'-lantern yet, have you?"

Mandy shook her head.

"Well, this is for you, then," he said, giving it to her. "A Halloween gift to welcome you to Chaldon Herring."

"Thank you so much," Mandy said.

"And here's a pumpkin pie my wife made," Tony said, taking a pie shell with bright orange filling from a glass case on the counter.

"It looks delicious," said Dr. Adam. "I can't resist a good pumpkin pie. What do we owe you?"

Tony looked taken aback. "Nothing! They're both welcome gifts."

When Mandy and her dad left the store, a young boy came out of a house on the other side of the road and waved to them. "Hello, Dr. Hope and Mandy."

"Hi, there," Mandy called back. This was a little bit like being famous! The boy must have seen their photo, too.

"I'm getting a new puppy tomorrow," said the boy. "A Jack Russell. Mom says we'll bring him to you for a checkup."

"Can't wait to meet him!" Mandy said.

Farther along the road, two men with fishing rods greeted them. "Foggy afternoon, isn't it?" said one. "I hope it clears up for you."

"Yes, it would be a shame to come here and not see any of the coast," said the other.

When Mandy and her dad continued on their way, she remarked how friendly everyone seemed in Chaldon Herring. "It reminds me of home," she said.

"Yes. Nice village, nice people," agreed Dr. Adam. He stopped. "But there's one difference." He pointed to a painted wooden sign hanging from a sturdy flint-and-brick building. "The local inn."

"We've got the Fox and Goose," Mandy said.

"Yes, but look at that name," said her dad. "The Smuggler's Barrel."

Mandy chuckled. "Oh, right. Smuggling isn't exactly a feature in Welford. I guess we're just too far from the sea."

Later that afternoon, when Jessame was getting ready to go home, Mandy went outside with her. Darkness was falling and thick mist was rolling in over the cliffs. From Lulworth, the foghorn's haunting lament echoed through the gloom.

"Another foggy night," said Jessame, tucking her scarf into her jacket. She climbed onto her bike. "See you tomorrow!" she called. She pedaled away and was soon swallowed up by the mist. Only her white jacket revealed that there was someone there.

And then, above the eerie siren, Jessame called out to Mandy from the darkness. "Watch out for the ghost!"

"Ghost?" Mandy echoed in surprise. Jessame didn't sound as if she was teasing, and it wasn't even Halloween yet. "What ghost?"

But Jessame must have been out of earshot because she didn't reply. The only sound was another spine-tingling wail of the foghorn.

Two

If there was a ghost, Mandy wasn't going to wait until the next day to find out about it. She decided to see if the book on local smugglers could tell her anything. But before she even opened it, her mom came into her bedroom. "You need to get ready, love. We're going out to dinner in a few minutes."

Mandy put the book down. "To the Gray Horse?" she asked hopefully.

"Yep. Jessame said Pala can come, too. Apparently, the owner of the restaurant loves dogs."

"Great," Mandy said.

A little while later, they were on their way. It was an

eerie journey along the narrow roads, made spookier by tall hedges looming out of the mist on either side. Down at Lulworth, the foghorn seemed to warn of more than rocky outcrops. Perhaps the Gray Horse restaurant had once been an ancient gathering place for smugglers. Was it now a rendezvous for their ghosts? Mandy shivered. After Jessame's warning, she imagined a dark, creepy place where shadowy shapes flitted along gloomy, narrow passages, and whispers hovered in the air.

"Here we are," said Dr. Adam, and out of the mist, lights appeared, welcoming them to a sprawling white building with several rows of cars parked in front.

It couldn't have been further from Mandy's expectations. Colored lights stretched along the eaves, and there was a terraced area with chairs and tables where people could eat on sunny days. On each side of the front door, wide bay windows looked out onto a garden. Through the windows, Mandy saw groups of people sitting around tables, laughing and talking, or studying the menu. When she climbed out of the Land Rover, she heard the cheerful sound of voices and caught a whiff of delicious food. There was nothing in the least spooky about the Gray Horse restaurant!

"I don't think any self-respecting ghost would be seen dead around here," Mandy said, and she wasn't sure whether she was relieved or disappointed. She looked up at a sign hanging from a horizontal beam above the door. It showed a gray horse rearing up, ridden by a black-cloaked horseman. Here, at least, was one thing that hinted at the dark history of the area.

Inside, a man came over to them at once. He was just a bit taller than Mandy but strongly built, and he had a broad friendly smile. "Ah, Dr. Adam, Dr. Emily, and young Mandy. Pala, too," he added, bending down to pet the spaniel who strained at the end of her leash to greet him. "Welcome, welcome. We hoped you'd come for a meal."

Mandy had stopped being surprised that people knew who they were.

"I'm Jeff Halliday, owner of the Gray Horse," the man continued. "The Carhills are good friends of mine."

"Tiny Farmer and Jessame both said we could get an excellent meal here," said Dr. Adam.

"The best in all of Dorset," Jeff promised, winking at Mandy.

A dozen framed pictures and faded newspaper articles hanging on the wall next to the door caught Mandy's attention. Looking closer, she saw that the pictures were drawings of tough-looking men, some of them in flowing black cloaks, and that some of the yellowing newspaper articles dated back to the eighteenth century. The headlines announced: HARRY DEFIES THE GOBBLERS and LANDSHARKS DEFEATED AT LULWORTH. They sounded like reports of soccer matches.

Jeff must have noticed Mandy's interest. "Have you heard of Harry Hawkins?"

She shook her head.

"He was one of the most notorious smugglers ever. Led the authorities on a lot of wild-goose chases for many years," said Jeff. "He and his gray horse, Cloud."

"The same horse this restaurant is named after?" Mandy asked.

"Yes. It's also where Harry was believed to hide out, in a secret room at the back of the cellar. Until . . ." Jeff paused, then said dramatically, "his last desperate chase across the Down."

"What happened?" Mandy gasped.

Jeff directed them to a table. "Take a seat, and I'll bring you a drink."

The place mats on the polished oak table showed smugglers rowing ashore or tying ropes around boxes of goods at the base of high cliffs. On the wall behind Mandy were more articles about Harry. Some were copies of the ones at the door, but there was a more modern-looking one. She was about to read it when Jeff returned with a tray of drinks, including a bowl of water for Pala.

He sat down opposite Mandy. "Harry Hawkins must

have landed hundreds of tons of illegal tea and silk on these shores, giving the gobblers and landsharks the slip every time by out-galloping them on Cloud."

Mandy frowned. "Gobblers and landsharks?"

"Smuggler jargon for customs officers," said Jeff. "But just when it seemed Harry was going to make another cunning escape, Cloud stumbled into a rabbit hole. Harry fell off and broke his arm, and Cloud broke his leg."

"Oh, no!" Mandy couldn't bear to think how, in the days before modern veterinary medicine, the brave horse would have been put out of his misery. Her dad must have guessed what was going through her mind because he reached across and squeezed her hand.

"So what happened to Harry?" asked Dr. Emily.

"He was found guilty and packed off to Virginia with lots of other convicts," said Jeff. "But he had the last laugh. He refused to tell the gobblers where his last haul was stashed until the ship pulled away from the dock. And then he shouted to the officers onshore, 'Ye'll find the crop . . .' — that's smugglers' lingo for cargo — '. . . in the secret chamber under the ground.'"

"And did they?" asked Dr. Adam.

Jeff shook his head. "No. In fact, they never found a secret chamber. If you're interested, after dinner I'll show you where the authorities bashed holes in the cellar walls all those years ago, looking for Harry's room. But it was all for nothing. No one knows where he put it." He signaled to a waiter to bring a menu.

Mandy used the pause in the conversation to scan the newspaper article on the wall behind her. It was dated just a few weeks earlier. The headline was intriguing. *"Harry and Cloud ride again,"* she read out loud.

"Ah, yes," said Jeff. "Harry and Cloud came back. But this time, as ghosts!"

"Really?" asked Dr. Emily, and Mandy could hear the skepticism in her voice.

"Yep," said Jeff, smiling his broad smile. "There have been regular sightings in the past few weeks of a ghostly gray horse ridden by someone wearing a long black cloak."

"Mmm, and pigs might fly," said Dr. Emily. "A tall tale perfectly timed for Halloween."

But Mandy was thinking of Jessame's warning. With stories of smugglers lost at sea, and the eerie feeling she'd had on the way here, she couldn't help feeling there might be some truth in the rumors after all. Perhaps Jessame had seen something spooky, too.

"It's probably just something made up by locals to tempt tourists," said Jeff in a more matter-of-fact voice. "And it's not that different from the stories the smugglers used to make up."

Mandy was puzzled. "Why would they want to trick people into coming here?"

"Actually, it was quite the opposite," said Jeff. "It was to keep people away, especially at night. You see, the smugglers wanted to move their cargo without being seen, so they spread gruesome tales of headless horsemen and nightmarish dogs running loose on Chaldon Down."

Mandy's mom laughed and opened the menu. "It shows how gullible people can be."

"And on misty nights like this, with the foghorn howling down in the cove, it's amazing what some folks see in the smallest shadow or the flutter of a leaf," said Jeff. He winked at Mandy who blushed, wondering if he'd guessed she was tempted to believe in the ghost. Jeff pushed back his chair and stood up. "Still, it's interesting that those who claim to have seen a ghost all describe the same thing: a big gray horse with a cloaked rider disappearing into the mist on the Down."

"Well, that's how rumors spread," said Dr. Adam. "Everyone jumps to the same conclusion just because they've heard someone else talking about it."

"Probably," agreed Jeff. "Now, if you'll excuse me, I must check that everything's all right in the kitchen. Enjoy your meal. I can recommend the Hearty Choke Pie if you're looking for something tasty to warm you up."

After Jeff left them, Mandy studied the menu. It was

hard to concentrate though, and her mind kept drifting to the legend of Harry and Cloud. "I wonder if there *is* any truth to that story?" she said after a while.

Dr. Emily raised one eyebrow. "Don't tell me you're falling for it, too. It's just a silly story."

Mandy decided not to argue, knowing her mom was probably right. She was just being overimaginative, thanks to a combination of Halloween and the eerie foghorn. She concentrated on the menu, eventually deciding on the Hearty Choke Pie. Apparently, the recipe came from a "recipe book" belonging to a Mary Pike. The note in the menu said that Mary was the wife of another smuggler, Isaac Pike.

"I'll have the same," said Dr. Adam. "You know what they say: When in smuggler country, eat like a smuggler."

The pie was a delicious concoction of artichoke hearts and tiny potatoes in a creamy cheese sauce. "Mary Pike certainly knew a thing or two about cooking," declared Dr. Adam.

Throughout dinner, Pala had behaved perfectly, lying quietly at Mandy's feet. But as Mandy finished her dessert she began to grow restless. "I'll take her out to stretch her legs," Mandy said.

"Stay in the parking lot," said Dr. Emily. "I don't want to send a search party out onto the Down for you."

Outside, the mist swirled around Mandy and Pala, and

the Lulworth foghorn sounded louder than before. Mandy shivered. Was it because of the cold dampness seeping in through her clothes? Or was it because of something more sinister? She looked at Pala to see if she'd sensed anything. Animals were supposed to be much more sensitive than humans toward supernatural things. Pala's nose seemed glued to the ground. She'd definitely sensed something. *Probably a rabbit trail,* Mandy thought, trying to ignore the jittery feeling she had.

Pala tugged at the leash, trying to go after the scent. Mandy let her go as far as the edge of the parking lot. "That's far enough, Pala," she said, remembering her mom's warning.

But Pala had other ideas. Surprisingly strong for her size, she forged ahead, springing over the low, split-pole fence so that Mandy quickly had to jump over it and run behind her. She glanced back to make sure she hadn't lost sight of the restaurant and the parking lot. The lights were burning brightly through the mist, and Mandy could still see the Land Rover so she felt safe to let Pala go on a bit farther.

Pala zigzagged ahead, sometimes doing a U-turn before turning sharply again to the left or right. After a couple of minutes, Mandy thought it was time to go back. "Heel, Pala!" she called. "That rabbit's probably miles away by now."

Pala stopped and stared straight ahead.

"What is it?" Mandy peered into the gloom. She thought she heard a muffled thudding, and she glimpsed something moving. "That's too big to be a rabbit," she murmured, and in that moment, the mist parted in front of her. If she'd glanced away, or turned back earlier, she wouldn't have seen it. But in the split second before the mist rolled in and closed the gap again, a gray horse appeared, cantering toward her with its tail flowing behind like a flag. And on its back, crouched low over its neck, was a rider wearing a long black cloak.

Three

"Mandy! Where are you?"

It was her dad, calling from the parking lot. She whirled around and raced toward the lights, Pala bounding at her side.

"Mandy?" yelled her dad again.

"I'm here!" Mandy called.

In the parking lot, she found her mom and dad, both looking furious.

"What were you doing out there?" Dr. Adam demanded. "You could have gotten lost."

"You were supposed to stay in the parking lot," said Dr. Emily.

"I saw the ghosts!"

"Likely excuse," said Dr. Emily. She put her hand on Mandy's back and guided her toward the Land Rover.

Mandy stopped and looked squarely at her. "It's not an excuse. I really saw them. A gray horse and a cloaked rider."

Dr. Adam laughed. "You've had a few too many stories today."

"That's got nothing to do with it," Mandy said. "I wasn't even thinking of ghosts when the horse and rider appeared. Pala saw them, too."

Dr. Adam unlocked the Land Rover. "Your eyes can play tricks on you in the mist, especially when it's dark."

"I know what I saw," Mandy said, but as they headed home, she began to have doubts. Her dad was right: Perfectly ordinary things could take on a new shape in fog. But after all the stories she'd heard, was it really just a coincidence?

I'll just have to find out for myself, she decided. *I'll take Pala for a walk across Chaldon Down first thing tomorrow to look for something to explain it all.*

The next morning, Mandy found a map of the area tucked in a drawer in the kitchen. It showed a footpath she could take straight across the Down to the Gray

Horse. From there, she'd retrace her footsteps to where she saw the mysterious vision.

She filled a thermos with hot chocolate and put it into a backpack along with a bottle of water and a small bowl for Pala, two apples, and a few dog biscuits. She clipped the leash onto Pala's collar and was on her way across the yard when a battered red Mini Cooper sped in through the gates and screeched to a halt outside the cottage.

A tall young man in a denim jacket and small gold-rimmed glasses jumped out from the driver's side. "Is the vet in?"

"Sure. What's the problem?" Mandy asked.

A passenger climbed out, too. She was a young woman with close-cropped auburn hair. "We've got an animal that's really sick," she said, folding the seat forward. She leaned into the back of the car and brought out a big cardboard box. "I hope the vet's not too busy to see us."

"Mom and Dad always treat emergencies immediately," Mandy said, leading the way inside.

Pala looked disappointed that her walk was coming to such an abrupt end. When Mandy put her into the utility room before going to the clinic, the dog barked at her in protest.

"Sorry, Pala. It's just for a few minutes," Mandy promised, shrugging off her backpack. She shut the door and ushered the new arrivals to the waiting room. "What kind of animal is it?" Mandy asked. From the size of the box, she guessed it was a cat or maybe a large rabbit.

Before anyone could answer, Dr. Emily came out of her treatment room to call in the next patient, a very healthy-looking sheepdog. It was the only other animal in the waiting room, and its elderly owner seemed to be having a hard time keeping it still.

"We have an emergency, Mom," Mandy said quickly, and she gave the dog owner an apologetic look.

"Oh, don't mind me," he said. "You go right ahead. Bounder isn't sick. He needs his shots, that's all."

"Thank you, Mr. Bugler," said Dr. Emily. "This way," she said to the young couple. "You come in, too, Mandy, in case I need a hand. Jessame is helping Dad with a difficult cat."

In the treatment room, Dr. Emily pointed to the stainless steel table in the middle of the room. "Put the box on there, uh . . ."

"Emma," said the woman, carefully resting the box on the table. "And this is Jay." She nodded to her partner.

Mandy, Jay, and Emma gathered around the examination table while Dr. Emily washed her hands at the sink. "So, what have we got here?" she asked, drying her hands.

Jay sounded embarrassed as he said, "We don't actually know."

"What?" Dr. Emily looked surprised. She dropped the paper towel into the trash and came over to the table.

"It sounds crazy," said Emma, "but, you see, it's not ours." She was easing off the lid of the box, which was punctured with air holes.

Mandy was intrigued. This was the first time anyone had brought in an animal they couldn't identify!

"We found it in our yard late yesterday," Emma went on. "We were going to contact a zoo about it today, but when we woke up this morning, it looked really sick." She lifted off the lid.

Mandy looked inside. "It's a baby dragon!" she exclaimed. There was no other way to describe it; the creature could have come straight out of the pages of a children's fairy tale. It was dark brown, about eighteen inches long, with a very long tail, scaly skin, sturdy legs with sharp claws at the end of each toe, big eyes, and a powerful-looking mouth that was so wide it stretched almost all the way around its face from one ear to the other. It almost looked like it was smiling.

"It's actually a giant lizard," said Dr. Emily. "You're right about it being a baby, though. And in a sense, I suppose it is a dragon. It's a *Komodo* dragon."

Mandy couldn't take her eyes away. "It's incredible!" she murmured.

"Komodos are very special," agreed her mom.

"They're the biggest lizards on earth. They can grow to be twelve feet long and can weigh up to three hundred pounds."

Emma looked stunned. "Three hundred pounds! That's more than me and Jay put together. And to think it showed up in our backyard."

"Where could it have come from?" asked Jay. "I mean, we don't have animals like that in England."

Dr. Emily pulled on some thick rubber gloves. "No, not living in the wild. This little guy is from Indonesia."

"Isn't that somewhere near Australia?" Mandy said, trying to remember from her geography classes exactly where Indonesia was.

"Yes," said her mom. "It's a group of islands spanning the equator."

Emma bit her lip. "Wow. How did it end up here?"

"That's what I'd like to know," said Dr. Emily, looking serious. "It's definitely not the kind of reptile one keeps as a pet." She reached into the box and stroked the lizard's scaly back.

There was no response from the Komodo, not even a warning hiss. Its build suggested that it was a tough, fast-moving creature, possibly quite aggressive. But it lay motionless in the box, its eyes sunken and half-closed, and its sides moving in and out with quick, shallow breaths.

"Poor baby," Mandy said. "What do you think is wrong, Mom?"

"I honestly don't know," said her mom. "I've never handled a Komodo dragon, and I know very little about them. Call Dad, please, Mandy."

Dr. Adam and Jessame were just as shocked when they saw the reptile. Jessame could only stare at it in stunned silence, while Mandy's dad demanded angrily, "What on earth are you two doing with a Komodo dragon?" He frowned at Emma and Jay. "Don't you know that CITES prohibits trade in these animals? They're extremely rare and endangered!"

Having had experience with other threatened animals,

Mandy was familiar with the term CITES. It was short for Convention on International Trade in Endangered Species.

"Spike's not ours," said Jay.

In spite of the seriousness of the situation, Mandy had to smile at the name. It was perfect for a scaly dragon.

"And we had no idea he was so rare," Jay continued, telling Dr. Adam and Jessame how he and Emma had found Spike in their backyard. "We really hope you can help him," he finished.

"Unfortunately, Komodo dragons are way out of our field," said Dr. Adam. "The best we can do is see to his immediate needs and contact a reptile specialist."

"There's a reptile center at Bournemouth Zoo," said Jessame. Bournemouth was a city on the coast about forty miles to the east. "I'll find the telephone number for you."

"I'll follow that up, Adam, if you'll take a look at Spike," said Dr. Emily, sliding her hand beneath the sickly creature. "Judging by the way he looks, I don't think we have a lot of time."

Mandy's heart lurched. Not much time to save the smiling lizard? "Then we shouldn't waste a minute!" she declared.

Four

While her dad examined Spike, Mandy and Jessame prepared a temporary home for him. Mandy knew that the Komodo dragon would need to be kept warm because like all reptiles, he was cold-blooded, which meant he didn't regulate his own internal temperature. Instead, he warmed up in hot environments and could get dangerously cool when it was cold. But would one of the cages in the residential unit be good enough?

"I have just the thing for him," said Jessame.

It was a heated glass tank. It was rectangular and about the size of a widescreen TV. "We bought it last spring to keep some orphaned kittens warm until we found them new homes," said Jessame. "Who would have thought we'd need it again for a giant lizard?"

They cleaned out the tank with disinfectant and lined it with newspaper. It looked bleak and unwelcoming compared with the other cozy cages for sick animals, so Mandy added a few stones and a small branch. "To make it a bit more homey for Spike," she explained, arranging them inside the tank.

"Speaking of home, I wonder how he ended up in Jay and Emma's yard?" said Jessame, switching on the heat lamp.

Mandy put her hand inside the tank, feeling the warmth seep in. "Do you think he could have escaped from a zoo?"

Jessame shrugged. "I'll call around and see if I can find out. It could be that someone near here has a private collection of exotic animals."

"Dad said Komodos aren't allowed to be sold, even to collectors," Mandy pointed out.

"Maybe he wasn't sold," said Jessame. "He could have been bred in captivity."

Even though this seemed possible, it still didn't make it right. Spike was thousands of miles from his real home, in a climate that did not suit Komodos. And on top of that, or maybe because of it, he was seriously ill.

Mandy was checking the temperature of the tank

again when Dr. Emily came in. "I've been on the phone with Tracy Parker. She's a lizard expert at the reptile center in Bournemouth," she said. "She was shocked to hear about Spike and would have come over right away. But she's giving an important lecture at a conference this afternoon so the earliest she can come is tomorrow morning." She looked approvingly at Spike's new quarters. "Perfect," she said. "Tracy said it was critical to keep Spike warm. Where should we put the tank?"

Jessame glanced at the other animals in the unit. "He needs to be kept in quarantine in case he's suffering from something contagious."

"You're right," said Dr. Emily. "Since we haven't the foggiest idea where he came from, we should be extra careful. If he was brought in from Indonesia and the sickness is something unique to the area, we could end up with a disaster on our hands. The local animals won't have any natural resistance to a new disease, and it could spread through them like wildfire."

Mandy imagined with horror an epidemic sweeping through the country, killing huge numbers of animals.

"I think I know just the place for him," said Jessame, pointing to a door at the end of the unit. "There's a cupboard in the storeroom through there. We could put the tank on one of the shelves."

The cupboard had deep, well-spaced shelves that

could easily accommodate the heated tank. It was also a quiet place where Spike would have some privacy. Mandy and Jessame were just clearing out the middle shelf when Dr. Adam, Emma, and Jay came through with Spike.

The Komodo lay limply in Dr. Adam's hands, like a bag of sand. Mandy bent down so that she was level with him. "You don't belong in England," she whispered. "You should be far away, with other Komodos, where it's warm and wild."

Whether it was just a coincidence, or whether Spike actually heard her, Mandy would never know, but he opened his eyes and slowly lifted his head until he was face-to-face with her. It was an extraordinary thing to look into the eyes of a giant lizard, and Mandy was tempted to stroke the top of his head, like she would have petted a dog or cat. She might even have done so if her dad hadn't stopped her.

"Careful, Mandy," warned Dr. Adam. "If Spike feels threatened, he could bite. Komodos' mouths are full of dangerous bacteria that can cause deadly infections."

Hearing this, Emma and Jay exchanged a worried look. "We're lucky he didn't give us a nip when we picked him up," said Jay. "We weren't even wearing gloves."

Mandy straightened up. She had a lot of respect for wild animals and would never willingly do anything

silly. Still, she didn't think Spike looked the least bit menacing. The expression in his dark eyes was more of a plea, like he was asking for help.

Spike closed his eyes and dropped his head back onto Dr. Adam's gloved hand. The lizard looked completely worn out. The effort of lifting his head must have cost Spike what little energy he had left.

"Have you figured out what's wrong with him, Dad?" Mandy asked.

"To start with, he's hypothermic, which means his

body temperature is very low," said Dr. Adam. "So we'll have to get that up. That tank should help a lot, but we could do with a heating pad, too."

"I think we have one," said Jessame, and she started to look inside the other cupboards in the storeroom.

"What else do you think is wrong?" Mandy asked.

Her dad traced his finger lightly down Spike's back. "See how wrinkly his skin is and how his eyes are sunken in? That means he's dehydrated and hypoglycemic."

Mandy knew that "dehydrated" meant Spike needed fluids. She'd already put a dish of water inside the tank, anticipating this. As for the other term, she wasn't sure she'd heard it before. "Hypo-what?" she asked, wrinkling her nose.

"Hypoglycemic," said her mom, "meaning low blood sugar. That would be because he hasn't been eating."

The solution to that seemed easy enough. "Then we'd better feed him," Mandy said. "What does he eat?"

"Raw meat," said Dr. Adam. "But I doubt he'll start eating on his own. We need to get his body temperature up first."

Jessame came back in with the heating pad, which looked like a miniature electric blanket. She put it in the tank and with the help of a heavy-duty, grounded extension cord, plugged it into a socket in the wall.

"In you go, Spike," said Dr. Adam. He lowered the

lizard onto the pad, then fit the glass lid on top of the tank.

"There, Spike, your own electric version of a sun-warmed rock," said Jay, looking at him through the side panel.

Spike didn't seem to care. He lay utterly still on the pad. Minutes ticked by, but the warmth made no difference. Mandy dug her fingernails into her palms. Her mom and dad were amazing vets, but even they couldn't always save an animal. Was Spike going to be one of those they couldn't help? "Perhaps we need to turn up the temperature," she suggested.

Dr. Adam shook his head. "No. It'll be warm enough. You must remember that cold-blooded creatures take longer to respond than warm-blooded animals. That's because their metabolism — and all the processes in their bodies — are so much slower than in warm-blooded animals. We won't see an immediate change in Spike."

This was little comfort to Mandy. There *had* to be more they could do. "Are you sure we can't feed him yet, Dad?"

"Let's give him a couple of hours to warm up. Then we'll try him on some liquid meat," said Dr. Adam.

It was frustrating for Mandy to leave Spike looking no better. Crossing her fingers that he'd at least take a few sips of water soon, she returned to the reception area with the others.

Mr. Bugler and his sheepdog were still there, both fast asleep. Mr. Bugler's head had dropped forward onto his chest, and Bounder lay curled up at his feet. But as everyone came in, they woke up. Bounder leaped up and put his front paws on his owner's lap while wagging his shaggy black-and-white tail.

"I like you, too, boy, but that'll do," said the old man, trying to push him away.

Mandy went to help. She held Bounder's collar and eased him off Mr. Bugler's lap. Bounder sat down at once.

"Thank you, dear," said Mr. Bugler. "You're good with dogs, aren't you?"

"And with dragons," said Jessame, smiling at Mandy. "I saw how Spike related to you."

Mr. Bugler looked baffled. "Dragons? Spike? It must be Halloween."

Mandy chuckled. "There really is a dragon called Spike." But when she added it all up — mysterious horses and riders materializing like ghosts out of the mist, terrified people reporting sightings of apparitions on the Down, and now a dragon appearing out of the blue — it did seem weird and completely appropriate for the spooky season.

Jay and Emma were about to go. "Thank you for taking in Spike so quickly," said Emma.

"We'll visit him later this afternoon," said Jay. "After choir practice."

Dr. Emily was ushering Mr. Bugler and Bounder into the treatment room. Jay's remark made her turn around. "You're singers?" she asked.

"Actually, music students," said Jay. "I play the clarinet, and Emma, the cello. But we sing, too, in the local choir."

"So do I," said Dr. Adam passing through.

"Hey, that's great!" said Emma. "Maybe you'd like to join us at the village hall later this week for an evening of folk songs and smugglers' ballads."

"We'd love to, wouldn't we?" said Dr. Adam, looking at Mandy and her mom.

"Sounds like fun," said Dr. Emily.

Mandy went out to the car to get some sheet music from Jay and Emma so that she and her parents could practice. One of the song titles made her laugh. "*The Ballad of Harry Hawkins*," she read. "The ghostly rider! I can't get away from him."

"What do you mean?" said Emma.

"I've heard so much about him since we arrived," Mandy said. "And last night, I might have even bumped into him. Or rather, his ghost."

Emma opened her brown eyes wide. "Really? Where?"

"On Chaldon Down," Mandy said. "He was riding Cloud."

Jay had gotten into the Mini Cooper. He was so tall his head touched the roof inside. He leaned out of the window, ducking to avoid bumping his head. "Are you sure it was Harry's ghost?"

"Who else?" Mandy said. "No real horse and rider would gallop across the Down that late on a dark and misty night."

"It is odd," Emma agreed. "It's almost worth going on a ghost hunt."

Mandy explained that she'd been about to do just that. "Then you brought Spike in, which was much more important," she said. "But I still want to go."

"Good luck!" Jay called as he started the engine.

As the sound of the car faded away, Mandy let Pala out of the utility room. The dog streaked out, barking with excitement. After telling Jessame where she was heading, Mandy set off across the Down, following a footpath marked by low stone markers. Pala raced ahead, her nose to the ground as she tracked another irresistible scent.

After about fifteen minutes, they came to a place set back from the cliffs, where the land ran down steeply into a hollow. A spring bubbled out from one end of the hollow and coursed along the ground for twenty yards before disappearing inside a dense tangle of brambles. A few hundred yards to the right of the dip stood the Gray Horse Restaurant. It was the only building in sight, looming above the Down like a lighthouse overlooking a flat green ocean.

I must have been near here last night, Mandy guessed, orienting herself by standing with her back to the parking lot.

Pala was scurrying in tight circles at the top of the hollow. Suddenly, with her nose close to the ground, she bounded down into the gully.

"Pala, come back!" Mandy shouted.

But Pala had already scrambled into the brambles.

Sighing, Mandy ran after her. A twitching branch on the seaward side pinpointed where the excited dog was. Mandy called her again, and a figure appeared from behind the tangle of spiny undergrowth.

It wasn't Pala. It was a young man.

"Oh!" Mandy said, startled.

"Hello," he said, finding a path around the brambles and coming toward her. He wore a waterproof jacket, close-fitting waterproof pants, and rubber shoes that looked like thin-soled sneakers. Mandy guessed he was hiking along the coast; he was certainly well-prepared for wet weather.

"Are you looking for something?" he asked.

"My dog," Mandy said. "She ran down here."

The man looked alarmed. "Call her back. She could get into trouble. It's a dangerous place, you know. You shouldn't have let her come here."

"I couldn't help it," Mandy protested and to her relief, Pala burst out from the brambles and raced over to her, giving her a broad doggy grin. "There you are!" Mandy said, grabbing her collar so she couldn't run off again.

"Lucky," said the hiker as he headed up the side of the gully. "Don't hang around too long. It isn't safe."

"Why not?" Mandy asked.

"Haven't you heard?" he said, looking back over his shoulder. "This is Spooky Hollow. Home of Harry Hawkins and Cloud."

Five

As Mandy stared at him in astonishment, the hiker scrambled up the last part of the gully and vanished over the top. "Quickly, Pala," she said, starting up the steep slope in the opposite direction.

It wasn't to avoid bumping into any ghosts; Mandy had just noticed it was almost noon. Her mom had said they'd see if Spike would eat some food at lunchtime, and Mandy didn't want to miss that.

Near the top, she paused, noticing a row of marks in the ground. *Hoofprints.* And they were going right through Spooky Hollow! She felt her spine tingle. "That *must* have been Harry and Cloud I saw last night. We'll just have to come back later."

She scrambled up the last few yards, grabbing onto clumps of bristly grass to stop herself from slipping back down. She'd just reached the top when something occurred to her. She looked behind her at the hoof marks. *Ghosts don't leave footprints!*

The trail must have been left by a real horse, but who would ride through a supposedly haunted hollow at night?

Back at the clinic, Mandy took Pala up to the apartment before going in to see Spike. She hoped that after nearly two hours in the warm tank, there would be some improvement in the Komodo's condition. But if he felt any better, Spike wasn't letting on. He was exactly where Dr. Adam had put him earlier, on his heating pad with his eyes shut.

Maybe it's still too soon, Mandy told herself as her mom and Jessame came in. They both wore gloves and Dr. Emily held some plastic tubing and a big syringe. Jessame was carrying a blender jug.

"What's on the menu for Spike?" Mandy asked.

"Liquid hamburger," said Dr. Emily, making a face.

While Jessame held Spike in an upright position, Dr. Emily put the tube in his mouth and gently worked it down into his stomach. "I'll hold the tube in place, Mandy, while you push some of the food into it," she said, handing Mandy the syringe.

Mandy had seen other sickly animals being tube fed, but never a reptile. She put the syringe into the end of the tube and carefully pressed down the stopper, making sure she didn't force the liquid meat down too fast.

After just one syringeful, Dr. Emily stopped Mandy. "That'll do for now," she said. "We shouldn't overfeed him." She pulled out the tube and washed it at the sink while Jessame put Spike back in his tank. "Now," said Dr. Emily, leaving the tube to dry on the drain board, "let's have our own lunch."

Having just seen liquid meat, Mandy had lost her appetite. "Uh, would you mind if I have mine later?" she asked. "I want to make some posters about Spike and put them up in the village, in case his owners are searching for him."

"It's worth a try," said Jessame. "I called all the zoos in Dorset and Devon this morning. None of them even keep Komodos."

"Then he must belong to a private collector," Mandy said. "All the more reason to make some posters."

She was in her room jotting down ideas for her poster when the phone rang. "It's for you, Mandy!" called her dad from the living room.

It was James Hunter, her best friend back home in Welford. He was a year younger than her, and as crazy about animals as she was. "You promised you'd call as soon as you got to Dorset," he reminded Mandy.

"That's right. I'm sorry. I completely forgot," she confessed. "There's been so much going on." She told him about Chaldon Herring, Pala, the clinic, the misty Down, the Lulworth foghorn, the Gray Horse, and then about the exciting things that had happened: Spike's arrival, Spooky Hollow, and the ghost of Harry Hawkins and Cloud.

James whistled softly. "You're lucky! Rare reptiles and smugglers' ghosts? Great Halloween stuff. I wish I were there."

"So do I," said Mandy. "You could come to Spooky Hollow with me tonight to see if anyone shows up." She spoke in a low voice, not wanting her parents to hear what she was planning to do.

"Are you going alone?"

"I'll take Pala with me," Mandy said. "But before then, I've got to make some posters about Spike and put them up in the village. They'd be better if I had your help. I'm no good at drawing giant lizards."

"Why draw Spike?" James sounded horrified. "This is the twenty-first century. Why don't you just take a digital photo and download it onto the computer? It'll take you five minutes. Unless . . . the Carhills' place is as old-fashioned as Animal Ark — with a computer from the Dark Ages."

Mandy laughed. "Great idea. I'll borrow Mom's digital camera. And even if the computer here can't handle photos, at least I'll be able to show you what Spike looks like."

The computer turned out to have everything Mandy needed to make the posters. After taking a few shots of Spike, she got to work. As James had promised, the posters were ready in no time. At the top, there was a bold heading in large capitals: KOMODO DRAGON FOUND. Beneath it was a big color photograph of Spike. Even though he was so sick, he was very photogenic and looked every inch a powerful and exotic carnivore. Below the photograph, Mandy gave all the details about him. Feeling proud of the finished product, she put the posters in an envelope and set off with Pala for the village hall. Judging from how many people had seen the Hopes' photograph there, it seemed to be the place locals went for information.

Inside the hall, a karate class had just begun. A woman was standing next to the bulletin board, helping her young son tie his belt. She greeted Mandy with a smile. "Hello. Did you come to watch the class?"

"Actually, I wanted to put this up," Mandy said, and held up the poster of Spike.

The woman and her son stared at it. "Wow! A crocodile," said the boy.

"No," Mandy said, "it's a very special lizard."

The boy's mother wasn't quite as impressed. "Just as well it's off the streets. I'd hate to bump into that on a dark night."

The grocery store was the next place on Mandy's list. Tony Farmer raised his eyebrows when he saw Spike's picture. "What a beauty! I'd love to have a pet like that."

"Actually, Komodo dragons don't make good pets," Mandy explained. "People aren't supposed to own them because they're endangered. And they're really dangerous."

"Dragons? Dangerous?" A woman about the same age as Mandy's grandmother had just come in. "Oh, dear. What next?" she gasped, staring in horror at the poster.

Mandy quickly reassured her. "You don't have to worry. He's safely . . ." She nearly said, "under lock and key," but it would sound like he was in jail.

"Safely where?" the woman prompted.

"In a closed tank inside a cupboard in a storeroom," Mandy said.

The woman breathed out in relief. "Oh, well. That's all right then, isn't it?"

"No, it isn't," Mandy said. "He's really sick. He should

be in Indonesia, not in an artificial environment because it's cool to have an unusual animal for a pet." The moment she said this, she regretted it. Only a minute earlier, Tony had said he'd love a pet like Spike.

But Tony was nodding. "Good point, Mandy. Animals aren't fashion accessories."

It was midafternoon by the time Mandy had finished distributing the posters. She'd put one up at the bus stop, another on a big oak tree outside The Grange, and the last two on the porch of The Smugglers' Barrel. She hurried back to the clinic, hoping to see some improvement in Spike. Instead, she found her dad and Jessame lowering him into a basin of water.

"What's going on?" she asked.

"I just remembered something I learned in vet college," said Dr. Adam. "Some reptiles have a mechanism to absorb fluid through their skin."

"It should help to rehydrate Spike, plus being in water might encourage him to drink," said Jessame.

Mandy was fascinated. "Your body is doing some of the work, Spike," she said, watching him lying in the water. "Now it's time you did something to help yourself, too. A sip of water would be a start."

She didn't expect any reaction from Spike so she was thrilled when he suddenly shot out his tongue. It only lasted a second, but in that moment, Mandy saw that it was long, yellow and, like a snake's, forked at the end. Apart from when he'd looked at her earlier, it was the first voluntary movement she'd seen him make. "Did you see that?" she said to Dr. Adam and Jessame. "He must be starting to feel better!"

"Honestly, I'll be fine, Mom," Mandy insisted. "And I'll take Pala with me."

"If you were twenty-two and you had a pack of blood-hounds with you I wouldn't let you go wandering around the cliffs after dark," said Dr. Emily.

Dr. Adam closed the dishwasher and turned to Mandy. "Even *I* wouldn't go out there on my own at night."

It was early evening, and the Hopes had just finished supper. Mandy wanted to go back to Spooky Hollow to find something that would explain the mystery horse. Her parents wouldn't hear of it, though. Frustrated, she slumped down in a chair and folded her arms. "What are you scared of? Harry Hawkins and Cloud? And if there is a ghost, what's it going to do to me, exactly?"

"You're being silly now, Mandy," said her mom. "You know you could get lost and it's very cold out there. We don't need you coming down with hypothermia, like Spike."

"Then come with me," Mandy said.

"On a night like this?" said Dr. Adam. "It's so misty out there I can barely see the light above the garage door. I'm staying put in front of a nice fire."

Outside, there was the sound of a car driving through the gate. "That must be Emma and Jay," Mandy said. "They said they'd come by to see how Spike's doing." She went downstairs to let them in. "It's good to see you, but there isn't a lot of change with Spike," she warned them.

"Then there's probably no point in disturbing him," said Emma. "We'll come back tomorrow."

"No, come up for a drink and some pumpkin pie before you go," Mandy said. She felt bad that they'd come out for nothing. Or had they? "Unless you'd rather join me on a ghost hunt."

"Sounds cool," said Jay, smiling. "When do we leave?"

"Just as soon as Mom and Dad say it's OK for me to go," Mandy said.

Mandy's parents still needed some persuading. "Like we explained earlier, anyone can lose their way," said her mom.

But after Emma and Jay had convinced the Hopes that they were familiar with the area, Mandy's parents said it was all right for them to go to Spooky Hollow. "But be back by ten o'clock," said Dr. Adam as they set off.

Jay had a powerful flashlight, and he carried a

backpack from Dr. Emily containing a thermos of hot chocolate, three slices of pumpkin pie, and water and dog biscuits for Pala.

"The most important piece of equipment," Mandy announced, clipping the leash to Pala's collar as they went out the door, "is this." She touched the dog's nose. "The best ghost sensor there is."

They took the same path Mandy had followed that morning. Mist swirled around like thick smoke in the beam of Jay's flashlight. Mandy realized that her parents weren't being overprotective. On such a foggy night, with visibility almost zero, Chaldon Down wasn't a safe place for anyone alone.

They couldn't have been very far from Spooky Hollow when Jay stopped. "Did you see that?"

Mandy felt a shiver of excitement. "What?"

"That shape. Over there," whispered Jay.

"I can't see it," said Emma.

"That's fine," said Jay mysteriously. "You'd be scared."

Mandy held her breath but nothing emerged from the gloom.

Jay spun around then and flipped the flashlight on under his chin. Weird shadows fell across his face making it look like a ghoulish Halloween mask. "It's the ghost of Spooky Hollow!" he cackled.

"Very funny, Jay," said Emma.

They continued along the path, but a noise on the left like a twig cracking made them stop dead in their tracks again.

"What was that?" asked Emma with a gulp.

Another crack and Mandy froze. At her side, Pala stiffened. Mandy gripped the leash tightly.

"Wait here," whispered Jay. "I'm going to check it out." Before Mandy and Emma could stop him, he slipped away from the path, taking the flashlight.

The black night engulfed Mandy and Emma at once, and the mist smothered the sound of Jay's footsteps. The only sign that someone was out there was the fading beam from the flashlight.

"He shouldn't have gone off on his own," Emma said nervously. "We'd better follow . . ." She broke off as they heard a loud *thud*, a cry, and then total darkness as the flashlight's beam was snuffed out.

"Jay!" called Emma.

To Mandy's relief, Jay's voice came through the mist, calm and clear. "I'm OK. I tripped over something, bashed my knee, and broke the flashlight."

"Wait there and we'll come and find you," said Emma. "Keep calling so we know which way to go." She left the path, quickly vanishing into the mist like Jay had done. "Stay close, Mandy!" she called.

Mandy started after her, but Pala wouldn't budge. She

whined and stared into the fog, unsettled, fully alert, like a dog who had seen a ghost.

"What's there?" Mandy asked, slackening the leash. She let Pala tug her forward until she realized they had nearly reached the edge of Spooky Hollow. The hiker's voice echoed inside her head: *This is Spooky Hollow. It isn't safe.*

A step forward, and then another, and just as Mandy saw the ground sloping away into the gully, a ghostly shape exploded out of the mist and headed straight toward her.

Six

The unearthly white shape surged forward. Tall, majestic, galloping hard, it was instantly recognizable. "Cloud!" Mandy gasped.

It flashed past her and Mandy felt the warmth from the horse's body, heard the thud of hooves striking the earth, and the rasping breath of a swift-moving animal. This was no ghost!

"Wait!" Mandy spun around and charged after them. Pala raced along next to her, barking. But it was no use. The horse and rider, tangible, solid, as real as Mandy and Pala, had vanished into the night.

Who were they? And what were they doing galloping across the Down in the dark?

"Mandy!" Emma's voice, small and distant, was frantic. It came from somewhere to the right, in the opposite direction the horse had gone.

"Over here!" Mandy yelled.

Calling to one another like three human foghorns, Mandy, Emma, and Jay finally found each other.

"Did you see it?" Mandy asked breathlessly.

"See what?" said Emma. "Don't tell me we missed the ghost."

"Yes. I mean, no. It was a real horse, with a real rider."

Jay gave her a sideways look as he put his broken flashlight in his backpack. "On a night like this? Are you sure?"

"Yes. It was so close I could have touched it. Didn't you hear the galloping?"

"No," said Emma. "But sound doesn't travel far in fog like this. Which way did they go?"

Mandy shrugged. "I didn't see. They disappeared. Just like the ghost rider last night."

"It sounds crazy to me," said Jay.

"Weird," said Emma.

"Yeah," Mandy agreed. "And things are getting weirder every day around here."

*   *   *

"Thank goodness you're all back safely," said Mandy's mom, "and that your knee is only bruised, Jay."

Without a flashlight to shine on the path and with Jay limping, it had taken Mandy and the others nearly an hour to get home.

"Did you see any ghosts?" asked Dr. Adam, giving everyone a mug of steaming hot chocolate.

"Harry Hawkins and Cloud didn't show up tonight," Mandy replied. "But a *real* horse and rider did. They galloped right past me."

Dr. Emily looked at her in alarm. "That's plain reckless. They could easily have crashed into you in the dark."

"Probably some silly Halloween stunt," said Dr. Adam. "Someone pretending to be Harry Hawkins."

Later, snuggled up in bed, Mandy pictured the mysterious gray horse and rider. She'd had only the briefest glimpse of them, and all she'd seen of the rider was a figure wrapped in a long black cloak. Just like her dad said, it was as if someone had deliberately dressed up as Harry Hawkins. Could it really have been a Halloween prank?

Mandy's eyelids felt heavy. She turned over, and tucked the bedspread more closely around her. Tomorrow morning, she'd go back to Spooky Hollow to look for clues that would solve the puzzle once and for all.

*   *   *

"He's beautiful!" Tracy Parker lifted Spike out of his tank. She was young with long blond hair pulled back into a ponytail. Beneath her protective plastic tunic, she was dressed in trendy jeans, high-heeled boots, and a long-sleeved red shirt. For someone who specialized in scaly creatures that looked like dinosaurs, she was unexpectedly glamorous!

"Do you think he'll be OK?" Mandy asked. She'd tumbled out of bed extra early that morning to check on Spike, hoping for a change overnight, but when she went into the quarantine room, she was disheartened to find him as listless as ever. She had watched him for a while, hoping for a sign — another flick of his forked tongue or a tiny movement of his head — anything that would show he was starting to respond. Only a faint pulse in his side showed that he was alive. Nothing seemed to be working: not the warmth, not the food, and not the bath. Their only hope now was the expert from the reptile center at Bournemouth.

"It's hard to tell what will happen at this stage," said Tracy, putting Spike on a table. She stepped back and looked at him. "Reptiles take a long time to respond to treatment. With his slow metabolism, it'll be at least a week, perhaps even two, before we know if he's going to survive."

"Two weeks! We'll be back in Yorkshire by then," Mandy said.

"Don't worry," said Tracy. "I'll keep in touch to let you know how he's getting along. And you must come to visit him before you leave." Wearing thick leather gloves, she examined Spike's skin, touching it lightly. "He's not dehydrated anymore," she said, "and that's probably because of the bath you gave him. Did you deworm him?"

Mandy was surprised. "I thought only farm animals and dogs and cats got worms."

"Everyone can get them. Even us," said Tracy, opening a sturdy cardboard box she'd brought with her. It had ventilation holes in the lid, and on the sides, large red letters warned that a DANGEROUS REPTILE was in transit. "Reptiles can get a nasty worm-related disease called coccidiosis," she explained. "We'll treat Spike for internal parasites just in case." She picked him up and put him in the box. "He's one lucky Komodo to have ended up with you. Some people might have wanted to keep him. Ignorance about animals like this is a serious problem for us. Last month, we had a complaint about lizards in someone's backyard. We went to investigate and instead of the small lizards we'd expected, we found a young crocodile squashed up in a ridiculously small tank."

Dr. Adam looked very annoyed. "Who in their right mind would keep a crocodile?"

"You'd be surprised," said Tracy. "And the thing is, when these animals become too big and too dangerous, people often just dump them. You know, pass the problem on to someone else." She picked up the box.

"I'll carry that for you," Dr. Adam offered.

They left the storeroom and went outside to Tracy's car. Mandy opened the door so that her dad could put Spike on the backseat.

"It puzzles me that people can get ahold of crocodiles, let alone rare animals like Spike," said Dr. Emily. "I mean, even if you could buy a Komodo dragon, you'd have to have a special permit."

"You're right," said Tracy, getting into the driver's seat. "But some people deal illegally in protected species. I'll inform the police about Spike in case there's something like that going on around here." She started the engine. "And I'll call you if there's any change, I promise."

Mandy looked through the back window. *Hang in there, Spike,* she willed him silently.

She had mixed feelings as Tracy drove off. She was sad to see Spike go; she'd have loved to watch him get better. At the same time, though, she was relieved. *He's in expert hands now,* she told herself.

Jessame had taken the day off to visit an aunt, so Mandy stood in for her during the clinic's hours. It was another hectic day with Mandy's parents treating conditions ranging from tonsillitis in a Great Dane to an upset stomach in a guinea pig. Near the end of the afternoon, a couple came in with a blue parakeet. They wanted its wings clipped. They looked shaken, and Mandy thought this was because they were anxious about the procedure. It wasn't until after Dr. Adam had clipped the bird's wings that the woman said to her husband, "I wonder if we've done the right thing, Stan."

He nodded. "You're thinking about that lizard we saw, huh, Madge?"

"I am," she said. "If he comes for Baby Blue, she won't be able to fly away now."

"What lizard?" Mandy asked with a sense of foreboding.

"We heard about the big one that escaped," said Stan. "And just this morning we saw one scuttle out from the shed when we got some logs."

Mandy traded a worried look with her dad.

"What did this lizard look like?" asked Dr. Adam.

Madge held her hands three inches apart. "He was about this big," she said. "And he was brown."

If Mandy had looked at her dad, she would have laughed out loud. It sounded like Madge and Stan had disturbed

an ordinary lizard, the sort of shy, harmless reptile that
lived all over the British Isles. She studied the bird in the
cage instead. "I don't think you have anything to worry
about," she heard her dad say, a telltale catch in his voice.
"What you've described is a harmless native lizard."

Mandy and her dad managed to keep straight faces
until the door closed behind Stan and Madge, and then
Mandy gave in to her laughter. "Imagine if *they'd* found
Spike," she said. "They'd have fainted from the shock."

After supper, Mandy's parents went to choir practice
with Jay and Emma. Mandy offered to stay at home to
wait for Jessame who was coming by to pick up a bag of
hamster food for a neighbor.

When Jessame arrived and Mandy opened the door,
Pala shot out into the yard. "Sorry, Pala, no ghost hunt
tonight," Mandy told her, watching her scamper across
the lawn, sniffing the invisible tracks left by visitors
to the clinic that day.

"What's this about ghost hunts?" asked Jessame on
the way to the wooden outbuilding where the food was
stored.

Mandy told her about the previous night's adventure
on the Down. "I couldn't believe it when I saw that horse
and rider," she finished.

"It sounds as bizarre as if they *had* been ghosts," said
Jessame, tucking the bag of food under her arm and

closing the door. "But then again, I'm about to ride off in the dark myself."

"It's a clear night and you're on a bike, not riding a horse across the Down in the mist," Mandy said, watching Jessame pull up the hood of her parka. "And one other thing: You're not wearing a smuggler's long black cloak."

Jessame grinned. "Now, that's a good idea. It would keep me warm on the way home."

After Jessame had pedaled away, Mandy called Pala but there was no sign of her. Mandy searched the yard and even went out onto the road, but with no luck. She had no choice but to go after her. She grabbed a thick jacket and flashlight and hurried onto the Down. She kept her fingers crossed that Pala hadn't gone back to Spooky Hollow. The hiker's warning that a dog could get into trouble there was still fresh in her mind.

She ran along the now familiar path and paused at the edge of Spooky Hollow, shining the flashlight into the gully below. "Pala!" she called.

There wasn't a whisper of wind, a flutter of grass, or the soft padding of a dog's footsteps. The only sound was the distant swoosh of the sea rushing over the pebbles at the bottom of the cliffs.

"Pala!" Mandy yelled again, her voice ringing out in the stillness like a bell.

Waves of mist cascaded down the far slope, shrouding the brambles in the dip like a soft veil.

Mandy turned to go back, but hesitated when she heard a rustling noise from the bottom of the hollow, like a dog bursting through thickets. Or struggling to get free!

She raced down the slope, slipping and sliding over the damp grass. She skidded to a stop at the bottom, not far from the brambles. She looked around and at that moment, she heard a thundering sound. Just as she realized this wasn't the sound of waves thundering against the cliffs, she saw a ghostly white shape emerge from the other side of the brambles. A horse and a cloaked rider! Moving swiftly away from her, the apparition seemed to glide up the other side of Spooky Hollow toward the footpath on the top of the cliff.

"Harry Hawkins!" Mandy burst out.

The horse sprang forward when it heard her, bolting up the slope and unseating the cloaked rider who tumbled to the ground, landing with a solid, unghostly *thud*.

A loud cry confirmed the rider was no ghost. Stumbling over the uneven muddy ground, Mandy charged around the brambles and started up the other side. The beam from her flashlight fell upon the rider who was struggling to get free of the heavy cloak.

Mandy was only yards away now. "Are you all right?" she called.

The rider shoved off the cloak and turned to face Mandy, who stopped dead in surprise. Standing before her was a girl, no older than she, wearing regular riding clothes that were now streaked with mud.

"We've got to catch Fabian!" the girl cried.

Seven

There was no time for explanations.

Mandy scrambled up the slope. The horse, magnificent and white against the smokiness of the mist, was no more than a bus length away, but he was dangerously close to the edge of the cliff. One wrong step and he'd fall down to where the crashing of the waves warned of deadly rocks below.

Fabian's rider caught up with Mandy. She looked as frightened as her horse. Her elfin face, framed by her short black hair, was as pale as Fabian's coat. "I've got to get him," she said, but before she could go forward, Mandy caught her arm.

"No. Let me." She pressed the flashlight into the girl's hand. "Stay here. Shine the flashlight so I can see where I'm going. And don't say a word." The girl seemed so frantic, her tone alone could spook Fabian even more.

Inching forward slowly, Mandy approached Fabian. "Here, boy," she crooned, stretching out her hand. In the beam from the flashlight, she saw the muscles in his shoulders quiver. His tail was kinked high over his back, and his nostrils were flared.

"It's all right, Fabian," Mandy said, her heart thumping. A step closer, then another. Fabian's breathing was fast and shallow, and his neck and shoulders were damp with sweat. "I'm not going to hurt you," Mandy promised, stopping for a moment to give him time to get used to her.

His ears flicked forward but as Mandy took a step nearer, they went back again. His head went up even higher and he looked down at her, the whites of his eyes still huge. A loud blast from the foghorn made him flinch. He stamped the ground.

"Keep still," Mandy implored him.

Again, Fabian's ears flicked forward and this time, remained there. Encouraged, Mandy edged forward. "Hi there," she said, resting her hand on his side. Fabian looked around at her. Mandy ran her hand up to his neck, feeling the thick ridge of muscle beneath his mane, known as a crest, that told her he was a stallion. "You had a big scare," she said, reaching for the reins. "But everything's all right now."

She kept on soothing him and when he reached around and blew on her fingers, she knew he was starting to trust her. "Let's go back," she said, and coaxed him away from the edge.

Despite Mandy's gentle handling, Fabian was still wound up. He bounced along on his toes next to her, jerking his head up. Mandy was just as nervous. The slightest thing — a false step, a sudden loud rustle, a breath of wind — could make him bolt again. Slowly, they moved toward the girl. With each step, Mandy felt Fabian's fear fading. The bouncy tiptoeing gave way to a normal stride and his breathing slowed. Gradually, he relaxed his head and neck, carrying them lower.

"Oh, Fabian," the girl said through tears of relief as she hugged the horse's neck. "I thought I'd lost you." She looked at Mandy. "Thank you so much. You were amazing."

"You *could* have lost him," Mandy said. "It's really dangerous riding in the dark and mist." She was aware that she sounded a lot like her mom and dad when they'd stopped her going out alone onto Chaldon Down.

"Not really," said the girl, still hugging Fabian. "We're

usually fine but something in the brambles spooked Fabian tonight."

Mandy frowned. "*Usually* fine? Does that mean you and Fabian come out here every night?"

The girl didn't reply. She was already leading Fabian back through the hollow. Mandy hurried after them. "Where are you going?" she asked. "Aren't you scared of the ghost?"

The girl stopped to pick up the cloak she'd dropped when Fabian bolted. "Oh, yes, the ghost." She laughed.

It was a hollow, scornful laugh. Everything came together in an instant for Mandy: the gray horse, the black cloak, the hoofprints. "There isn't a ghost, is there?" she said. "It's *you!*"

The girl said nothing. She continued through the gully and up the far side to a thicket of trees at the top. Mandy followed her and was surprised when they came to a broken-down wooden shed hidden in the grove.

"What's going on?" Mandy said as the girl pushed open the crooked door and led Fabian inside. In the beam of the flashlight, Mandy saw that the ground was covered in straw. A feed bag hung on the back of the door, and there was a bucket of water in one corner and bales of hay against the wall.

"It's very complicated," said the girl, shutting the door and tossing the cloak into a corner. She started unbuckling the saddle. "Promise you won't tell anyone that you saw me."

Mandy's concern was growing. "Did you run away from home?" she asked, undoing Fabian's throat lash and noseband, and slipping the bridle over his ears.

The girl shook her head. "It's not that."

"Then what is it? Who are you? Where do you come from?"

The girl tousled Fabian's mane between her fingers. "My name's Paige Cleary. I live in West Chaldon on the far side of the Down."

"Why do you keep Fabian here?" Mandy asked. "And why do you ride at night? Do your parents know?"

Mandy must have hit a nerve because Paige blurted out, "I didn't steal him!"

"Whoa!" Mandy said. "I didn't think you were a horse thief. Just that something serious must have made you bring Fabian here."

"I promised someone I'd take care of him," Paige said quietly. "You see, uh . . . What's *your* name, by the way?"

"Mandy Hope." Waiting for Paige to continue, Mandy stood back to admire Fabian. Even in the meager beam of the flashlight, he was very handsome. He wasn't very tall, probably only a little more than fourteen hands, but he looked strong and capable of great speed. His ears were small and neat with tips that curved in toward each other, and his coat was a mix of white and dove gray, like sun-bleached pebbles. His neck was arched and his face had a concave or "dished" shape, which, along with the high set of his tail, helped identify his breed. "He's an Arabian, isn't he?" Mandy said, hoping this would encourage Paige to tell her more.

"Yes, he is," Paige said, opening a plastic grooming kit. She took out a wide-toothed plastic comb and began to untangle Fabian's mane.

"I'll give you a hand," Mandy offered. She chose a soft body brush from the kit and started to brush Fabian, holding the flashlight in one hand. Running the brush down a front leg, she felt him flinch. "What's the matter, boy?" she murmured, shining the beam down his leg. "Uh-oh," she said, seeing a blood-encrusted gash on his fetlock. "He's cut himself, probably from overreaching when he bolted." Overreaching was when a horse clipped its front hooves with the tips of its hind shoes. It was quite common during uncontrolled gallops over tricky ground.

Paige knelt down to inspect the injury. "Now what will I do?" she muttered, more to herself than to Mandy.

"We'll clean it first to see how bad it is," Mandy said. "If it's serious, we'll have to get my mom and dad to have a look at it. They're vets."

Paige's eyes opened wide. "No! No one can know I've brought Fabian here."

"Someone will have to if he needs treatment," Mandy said. She found a sponge in the grooming kit and a small bowl that she used to scoop some water out of the bucket. Sitting on the ground next to Fabian, she washed the wound while Paige stroked Fabian's neck.

"Luckily, it's only a small cut," Mandy said. Paige looked relieved, but her face dropped when Mandy added, "But it could get infected."

"So it *will* have to be treated?" asked Paige.

"Yes, and you really should take him back to his stable," Mandy said. She looked around at the ramshackle shed. "This is no place for a horse. It's too small and damp. And it must be very lonely."

"I know all that," said Paige, and Mandy heard a catch in her voice as if she was fighting back tears. She turned away. "But I don't know what else to do."

Outside, the wind blew through the trees, making them creak and groan. A tapping on the door startled Mandy until she realized it was just an overhanging branch. "Look, Paige," she said. "I want to help you. But you're going to have to tell me what's going on."

Paige bit her lip then took a deep breath. "OK, here's the story. Fabian isn't mine. But I've known him his whole life — he's six now. He belonged to an elderly man

named Abraham Trim. They lived on a farm just outside West Chaldon." She took a handful of pony nuts out of her pocket and gave them to the stallion. "I went there every day after school to help Abraham with his chickens and with grooming Fabian. And because Abraham was too old to ride, I always exercised Fabian."

Mandy smiled. It was exactly what she'd have done, too.

"Then, just a few weeks ago . . ." Paige swallowed before continuing in a sad voice, "Abraham died."

"Oh, no," Mandy said, feeling an ache in her heart. She stroked Fabian's arched neck. "You poor boy. Losing a person who must have meant so much to you."

"That's why I had to bring him to Spooky Hollow," said Paige. "Abraham had no family, and I was scared someone would take Fabian away and I'd never see him again. . . ." The words tumbled out in a rush, as if she were desperate to convince Mandy she hadn't done anything wrong.

"But you can't expect to keep him hidden forever!" Mandy said.

"That's why I only ride him at night," Paige said. "I thought the ghost rumors would keep people away after dark." She smiled wryly. "Except they didn't stop you."

"I was fooled at first," Mandy admitted. "Mainly because of the cloak, I think."

"I made it from an old curtain, so that people would think I was Harry Hawkins," said Paige.

Mandy remembered Jeff Halliday's accounts of customers arriving at the restaurant, scared out of their wits. "It worked on other people," she said. "There were even some articles in the papers about Harry and Cloud coming back."

"Yeah, Mom showed me those," said Paige. "I didn't know what to say. I didn't want to lie to her but I couldn't tell her the truth, either. If she finds out, she won't let me keep Fabian because we don't have much money, and we don't have any land of our own."

Mandy understood Paige's dilemma. To have to give up a much loved animal was one of the hardest things. Still, Paige couldn't continue like this. Even if Paige genuinely believed that she hadn't stolen Fabian, Mandy had a suspicion that grown-ups wouldn't see it like that. Also, Paige and Fabian could get hurt if they kept on with their night rides. Mandy shivered at the memory of the waves crashing below the sheer cliff. "You'll *have* to tell your mom," she said at last.

"I can't," Paige insisted. "She'd be furious if she knew I was riding out here at night."

"I bet," Mandy said. "My mom and dad would be mad if they knew I was out here now, too." She shone the flashlight onto her watch. "Shoot, they'll be home soon. I have to go."

"What are we going to do about the cut on Fabian's leg?" asked Paige anxiously.

Mandy hadn't forgotten about it. "I'll borrow some antiseptic powder from the clinic and bring it here in the morning."

"Thanks, Mandy," said Paige, picking up a blanket and draping it over Fabian.

"But you must promise me something, too," Mandy continued.

"What's that?" Paige asked as she stretched the blanket along Fabian's back.

"That you'll tell your mom everything."

"I can't," came the stubborn reply. "Not until Fabian's somewhere safe, where he won't be sold. But I don't know anywhere to take him."

"Then we'll just have to think of something," Mandy said. "Let's meet at ten tomorrow morning. We'll treat Fabian's cut and figure out a plan."

They went their separate ways, Mandy to the east and Paige to the west. The mist was thicker and Mandy was relieved not to have to worry about bumping into any ghosts. She was glad that she had the flashlight, especially since she didn't have her trusty tracker dog with her.

"Pala!" Mandy spun around and started back toward Spooky Hollow. She'd only gone a few yards when the flashlight dimmed, flickered, then went out altogether. The batteries were dead. She'd have to go back to the clinic for new ones. Luckily, it wasn't far. She took a shortcut over the back fence and was running past the wooden outbuilding where the animal food was stored when she heard frantic scratching behind the door — the sound of a dog's nails on wood. "Pala!" Mandy did a sharp U-turn and flung the door open.

Pala bounded out and leaped into her arms, bowling her over.

"Oh, you poor thing!" Mandy gasped. "You must have gotten shut in when Jessamc and I got the hamster food!"

Pala could not stop licking Mandy. "OK, OK. I'll make it up to you somehow." Mandy laughed, pushing her off and sitting up just as a pair of headlights swung through the gates.

It was Mandy's parents, and they were clearly surprised to find Mandy sitting on the ground in the dark.

"Out so late?" Dr. Adam said.

"I've been looking all over for Pala," Mandy said. "And all along she was right here."

"Sounds like you had a busy time," said Dr. Emily.

"Hectic," Mandy said, looking across to Chaldon Down. She was desperate to tell her parents about Fabian and Paige, but she'd promised not to. The secret of Spooky Hollow would have to come out eventually, but for now, the ghosts of Harry Hawkins and Cloud would continue to cover up for Paige and her beloved stallion.

Eight

Mandy arrived at the makeshift stable a few minutes before ten the next morning. It was a relief to get inside, out of the icy wind. Paige wasn't there yet. Fabian eyed Mandy warily.

"Don't you remember me?" Mandy said, pushing off the hood of her raincoat and holding out her hand.

Fabian stretched his neck and blew on her fingers, his breath warm and soft.

"Of course you do." Mandy smiled and stroked his face. He took a step back, still wary, and looked down at Pala who was standing quietly at Mandy's side.

"Pala's a friend, too," Mandy said. She knew that

although stallions had a reputation for being difficult, they responded well to confident handling and a calm voice. "Things have been crazy for you lately, haven't they?"

Fabian flicked his ears and looked at Mandy with an intelligent expression, like he understood what she was saying. Mandy rested her face against his neck, breathing in the warm fragrance of horse and hay. She couldn't help feeling envious. It would be thrilling to own any horse, but a gorgeous stallion like Fabian would be a dream come true. Arabians were her favorite breed, especially the stallions because of how closely they bonded with their human companions.

Suddenly, Fabian pulled away and stared at the door. Mandy hadn't heard a thing, but she guessed that the stallion had sensed Paige arriving.

"Hi, Mandy," said Paige, coming in, her cheeks flushed from the chill outside. She closed the door quickly, blocking out the icy wind, and went straight to Fabian. "How's my best boy this morning?"

Fabian nuzzled her head, blowing soft puffs of breath into her hair while she stroked his mane.

"Sorry I'm late," Paige said, looking around at Mandy. "I had to be very careful in case someone saw me."

"Same here," Mandy agreed. "But I guess most people wouldn't want to come all this way on such a miserable day." Then she remembered the hiker. "There *was* someone here the other day, though." She told Paige about him.

Paige looked worried. "Do you think he saw the stable?"

"Probably not," Mandy said. "He was across the Down. It looked like he couldn't wait to get away, like he believed the place is haunted."

"Let's hope everyone else thinks so, too," said Paige.

"We can't count on it," Mandy said. From her raincoat pocket, she took the jar of antiseptic powder she'd taken from the stock cupboard that morning. She'd felt bad about taking it without asking permission first, but she was going to pay for it out of her allowance. Kneeling down, she lifted Fabian's injured foot and carefully sprinkled some of the powder onto the cut fetlock. "You'll have to do this twice a day until the cut heals," she told Paige.

In the daylight, it was easier to examine Fabian properly, and Mandy saw that his hooves needed trimming and that he had no shoes. His coat was on the thin side, too, and dull.

"What's the matter?" asked Paige anxiously.

"He's not in great shape," Mandy said, standing up.

Paige put a protective hand on Fabian's back. "What do you mean? He's got food, and I groom him every day, and ride him whenever I can."

"I know you're doing your best," Mandy said. "But like I said yesterday, it's not a good idea to keep him here, especially with winter coming. He needs a thick straw bed, and indoor and outdoor rugs." She ran her hand across his side, feeling his ribs and hips protruding beneath his sparse coat. "And he needs hard feed, not just hay."

"I know all that," said Paige. "It's just that I don't have a choice."

"Take him back to the farm," Mandy said. "To his own stable."

"No!" Paige's eyes flashed. "He can't go back there. I'll lose him."

"But he's not yours, Paige," Mandy pointed out gently.

"Abraham always used to say Fabian was more my horse than his, you know," Paige replied. "Once he had to go to the hospital for two nights and he made me promise that whatever happened, I'd take care of Fabian." Tears welled up in her eyes. "I want to care for him for real, but Mom heard that Abraham's farm and everything on it is going to be auctioned. That includes Fabian!"

Mandy was silent for a moment. She could see that Paige was desperate to keep Fabian, and she felt truly sorry that Paige might be about to lose her beloved stallion. But Fabian didn't belong to her, and whoever owned Abraham's farm now must think he'd been stolen. There was no way Paige could keep Fabian like this — but more importantly, there was no way she could keep him here in this cramped, uncomfortable stable. Maybe it wasn't the right time to force Paige to give Fabian back, but Mandy could certainly help her find a better place to keep him. And if they found a good home for him, Paige's mom might consider buying him at the auction.

"We've got to find a new place for him," Mandy said, deciding she'd avoid the trickier issue of Fabian not belonging to Paige for now. "Come home with me for lunch, and afterward, we'll start looking."

Back at the cottage, she introduced Paige to her parents and Jessame, saying they'd met on the cliffs. *Which is true*, Mandy told herself. When everything with Fabian was figured out, she'd tell them the whole story. After lunch, riding bicycles they'd found in the garage, they went in search of a better home for Fabian. Their first stop was Misty Vale on the way to West Chaldon, the stables where Paige had learned to ride.

But the new owners of Misty Vale, Brigid and William Cobham, couldn't help them. The stables were full, and even if there had been space for Fabian, Brigid said they wouldn't have taken him in. "Stallions are too troublesome," she said.

"So that's that," said Paige gloomily as she and Mandy pedaled away. They rode through West Chaldon and toward another village called Owermoigne Galton. On the way there, they passed a young man putting up a sign next to a farm gate. It was only when she'd ridden past the sign that Mandy registered what it had said: MIDDLE FARM. STABLES AVAILABLE.

She braked so sharply she nearly somersaulted over the handlebars. "Hi there!" she called to the man, twisting around.

He looked over his shoulder at her. A few nails stuck out of the corner of his mouth. He took them out and said, "Hello!"

Paige had braked a few yards ahead of Mandy. Her face lit up when she read the sign. "It must be a new yard," she said.

"It is," said the handyman. "Are you looking for a stable?"

"Yes," Mandy said.

"Then go on up to the house and speak to Mrs. Broadbridge," he said, putting the nails back into his mouth.

"Broadbridge?" Paige echoed. "As in *Jemima* Broadbridge?"

The man nodded. "You know her?" he said, keeping his lips tight so the nails wouldn't fall out.

"Not exactly. But I've heard of her," said Paige. As she and Mandy rode through the gates, she explained that Jemima was a top cross-country rider. "I'd love to do that, too," she said wistfully, "with Fabian."

They cycled up to a modern-looking farmhouse with white walls and a black-tiled roof. A woman dressed in jodhpurs, ankle-length boots, and a green sweater was just going inside. She stopped on the doorstep when she saw Mandy and Paige and greeted them with a smile. "Welcome to Middle Farm," she said. "I'm Jemima Broadbridge. Can I help you?"

Mandy already had a good feeling about the place. "We're looking for a stable," she said.

Jemima's smile widened. "Well, you've come to the right place! Let me show you around."

Leaving their bicycles at the back door, they followed her to the stable. It was a brand-new building with a high-pitched roof. Inside, it was light and airy, and there were two rows of spacious stalls on either side of a wide aisle.

"This is great," Mandy said, comparing it with the meager shelter at Spooky Hollow. "Wouldn't Fabian just love it here, Paige?"

"He would," said Paige. She sounded oddly flat.

They went outside and crossed a yard to another, smaller stable. It wasn't a brand-new building but it was spick-and-span all the same. And, unlike the other, it was occupied. Two horses — both pitch-black thoroughbreds — peered over their stable doors at the visitors.

"My own horses," said Jemima, going to the first one and rubbing its cheek. "This is my mare, Moonshadow, and he," she nodded to the other horse three stalls away, "is my old boy, Midnight. He's retired now, but in his time he was the best cross-country horse in the county. He was a sought-after stud horse, too."

Mandy's heart skipped a beat. Stud horse meant

stallion! "Are you going to take in other stallions?" she asked.

"Well, I could," said Jemima, and Mandy shot Paige a hopeful look. "Do you two have a stallion?"

"Yes," Mandy began, but Paige interrupted her.

"Actually, we're not ready to move him yet," she said. "We're just looking at what a stable will cost."

"Let me give you a brochure. You can take it home and discuss it with your parents," said Jemima.

Mandy and Paige didn't wait until they were home to study the leaflet. A hundred yards from Middle Farm, they stopped on the side of the road. Mandy opened the brochure and the two friends pored over the details. The farm offered both full-time and part-time stables. Full-time meant that a horse was cared for completely by the yard owner. For part-time, the horse's owner did half of the daily routine. That involved going to the yard every morning or afternoon to feed, groom, and exercise the horse, muck out the stable, change the rugs, and either bring the horse in at night or let it out into the field in the morning. There were different fees for the two options. To Mandy, both seemed like a lot.

Paige looked at the prices and sighed. "It's what I thought. There's no way Mom and I could ever afford this. I thought I might have a chance at the other stables, but this would be like putting Fabian into a five-star hotel!"

Dejected, the two friends returned to Chaldon Herring. "We'll just have to keep looking," Mandy said when they'd returned their bikes to the shed.

"I guess," said Paige. "But I don't think we're going to find a place I can afford *and* will take in a stallion."

Later, after Paige had gone home, Mandy took Pala into the garden. "Fetch!" she said, tossing a tennis ball across the lawn. It was as much for her benefit as for Pala's; she had to do something to take her mind off Fabian, shut up alone in that miserable shed at Spooky Hollow. But even though Pala raced after the ball as fast as a dart and brought it back every time, Mandy couldn't cheer up.

"What are we going to do, Pala?" she sighed, gazing over the fence at Chaldon Down. "Poor Fabian. He must think he's been abandoned, even though Paige is doing everything she can for him." Thinking of an animal taken from its home reminded Mandy of Spike. He was in a better environment now, but was he still so ill?

Feeling even more depressed than before, she took Pala inside.

"Everything all right, honey?" asked her dad. "You look as if you've got the world on your shoulders."

"Any news about Spike?" Mandy asked.

"Funny you should ask," said Dr. Emily. "Tracy called while you were out. She invited us over tomorrow. We've rearranged the appointments so that we can take the morning off."

"Great!" Mandy said. She went to the kitchen to feed Pala. Watching the dog eating her supper, she wished Fabian could be in such a warm and loving environment. "And he will be," she said out loud, so that Pala looked up at her. "We *will* find him a new home!"

Early the next morning, Mandy took Pala for a walk. She was just going back indoors when she heard the squealing of tires. She looked around and saw the mailman's van screeching to a halt.

The mailman leaped out, holding a bag. "Is the vet in?"

"Yes. What's up?" Mandy asked.

"I'm afraid it might have died!" the postman exclaimed, thrusting the bag at her. "I hit it with my van."

Feeling the blood drain from her face, Mandy took the bag from him. Her heart pounded as she looked inside, expecting to see the lifeless body of a beloved cat or dog. But the creature inside was neither furry, nor cuddly. It was gray-brown, scaly, and wrinkled. Another giant lizard!

Nine

"Mom! Dad! Come quickly!" Mandy shouted.

"What is it?" called Dr. Adam, and Mandy heard him clattering down the stairs.

"Another lizard," she said as her dad arrived with her mom behind him. "But this one didn't make it."

The mailman looked dismayed. "I didn't mean to hit it."

Dr. Emily took the poor creature out of the bag and put it on the hall table. The prehistoric-looking body was rigid. Even so, it was an awesome creature. It was about twenty inches long and its stocky shape, large head, stubby legs, and strong-looking tail hinted that, like Spike, it was adapted to a special environment. A spiny crest ran down its back, and its face was short with a stumpy nose and mouth a bit like a beak.

"It must have been beautiful when it was alive," Mandy said sadly. "What kind of lizard is it, Mom?"

Dr. Emily shook her head. "I don't know. Do you, Adam?"

"Never seen one before, not even in a book," said Dr. Adam. "We'll take it to Bournemouth. Tracy might be able to identify it."

"Maybe it's endangered, too," Mandy said.

"Endangered!" echoed the mailman, looking even more unhappy. "And to think it's my fault it died."

"When did you hit it?" asked Dr. Emily.

"Ten minutes ago."

Mandy's mom raised her eyebrows. "Then you couldn't have killed it, Mr. um . . ."

"Tom Frewin," said the mailman. "But what do you mean? I didn't see it until it was too late to brake."

Dr. Emily turned the lizard over. "It was already dead. It's body is so stiff, it died at least three days ago."

"Really?" said Mr. Frewin, and Mandy saw some of the guilt drain from his face. "But it's a small consolation," he continued. "I mean, someone killed it, right?"

"There are no obvious injuries on its body," said Dr. Adam. "If it had been struck while it was alive, it would have been in a much worse condition. My guess is that it died from hunger, cold, or dehydration."

The mailman looked at the lizard as if he were seeing it for the first time. "So what happened? And where did it come from?"

Dr. Adam sighed. "That's the million-dollar question."

"This is tragic!" Tracy Parker exclaimed, holding the lifeless body as tenderly as if it were still alive. "It's a critically endangered species, as threatened as Spike."

"What kind of lizard is it?" Mandy asked.

They were in Tracy's office in Bournemouth. Pictures of reptiles covered the walls, but Mandy hadn't spotted one that looked like the dead creature Tom Frewin had found.

"It's not a lizard," said Tracy. "It's a tuatara, or, to be scientific, a *Sphenodon punctatus*. It belongs to a different line of reptiles altogether, the Sphenodontidae family. What makes tuatara really important is that they're the only surviving species of Rhynchocephalia. You've heard of the Jurassic era, haven't you?"

Mandy nodded.

"Well, Rhynchocephalias flourished then," Tracy explained. "And this one is the spitting image of its ancestors that roamed parts of the planet two hundred million years ago."

Mandy was speechless. She was looking at a twenty-first-century dinosaur! She hoped she'd remember all the details and the long names so she could tell James.

"Aren't tuatara from New Zealand?" asked Dr. Adam.

"Yes, but millions of years ago they lived in Europe, too, perhaps even along this very coast," said Tracy, taking a tape measure out of her desk drawer. "Now, they're found on only about thirty small islands off the New Zealand coast." She stretched the tape from the tip of the tuatara's nose to the end of its tail. "This one's no baby, like Spike. It must be nearly twenty years old."

"How can you tell?" Mandy asked.

Tracy put the tuatara inside a box on her desk. "Well, it's twenty-two inches long and they grow to a maximum of twenty-four inches. But they take about twenty years to mature," she explained. "In the right conditions, they can live up to a hundred years."

Mandy was shocked. Had the tuatara been in captivity in Dorset for decades? If that was the case, why had it been out on the road? Unless . . . "Maybe its owner died recently," she suggested, thinking of Abraham and

Fabian, "and whoever took it didn't care for it well and let it escape."

"It's not impossible," said Dr. Adam. "But I think there's a different explanation. Smugglers."

Dr. Emily nodded. "It looks as if Chaldon Herring could be the center of a reptile-smuggling racket. It's too much of a coincidence to find the tuatara and a Komodo dragon roaming around loose in such a short space of time. It's illegal to trade them, so criminals will find alternative ways to bring them into the country, like along empty stretches of coastline."

So smuggling was still very much alive in Dorset! But when it involved living creatures that probably suffered horribly during their ordeal, Mandy no longer found it as exciting as she had at first.

"There's a thriving black market in reptiles," Tracy agreed. "Komodo dragons and tuatara command huge sums. I'll contact the police again and give them all the details, as soon as we've done a postmortem to find how this animal died."

"Could it have been hypothermia, too?" Mandy asked.

"More likely dehydration," said Tracy. "Tuatara don't need as much warmth as other reptiles. They're nocturnal and their body temperature is very low so they can live normally in quite cold conditions."

After Tracy had given the tuatara to a colleague to do the postmortem, she took the Hopes to see Spike. On the way, they passed tanks containing fantastic-looking reptiles from all over the world. There were chameleons so well camouflaged they could have been leaves or sticks, and lizards that could make themselves look much bigger to frighten off their enemies. One of these was an Australian frilled lizard that unfolded a huge collar around its head. "It looks like an Elizabethan collar," Mandy commented.

Spike was in a roomy glass tank in the hospital section. He was lying on a wooden shelf with his eyes closed. Mandy felt a stab of disappointment. "He hasn't changed," she said.

But suddenly, Spike opened his eyes, lifted his head and stared straight at her.

"Hi, Spike!" Mandy said, bending down so that she was eye-level with him through the glass. "How are you doing?"

Spike flicked out his forked tongue, tasting the air in front of him and, to Mandy's delight, edged forward a little way before lying down again.

"Oh, wow!" Mandy said.

Tracy was just as thrilled. "That's the first time I've seen him move. If he keeps this up, we'll see if we can get him back to Indonesia."

Mandy hoped this didn't mean he'd end up in a zoo. "Will he go back to the wild?" she asked.

"That would be the idea," said Tracy. "There's a national park on Komodo Island where about a thousand other Komodos live. Some have been rescued, but most of them have always been there. It's the only place Komodos occur naturally, apart from a few smaller islands in the region."

"Perfect!" Mandy said.

"I think we should celebrate with some milk and cookies in the staff room," said Tracy.

Mandy stayed behind for a few moments after the others had gone out. She touched the glass tank, running her hand along the side, the closest she could get to stroking Spike. "Good-bye, beautiful Komodo dragon. And keep fighting so that you can go home where you belong."

In the staff room, Tracy introduced the Hopes to one of her colleagues, Andy Richards, who was a snake specialist.

"You're the vets who saved Spike's life?" said Andy, looking up from a backpack he was unpacking.

"I wish we could have done the same for the tuatara," Dr. Emily said somberly.

Andy nodded. "It's a shame about that one. Let's hope the cops find out where these reptiles are coming from."

He unpacked a pair of sneakers and tossed them onto a chair.

Thin-soled and made of rubber, the sneakers looked familiar to Mandy. The man she'd bumped into at Spooky Hollow had been wearing them. "Those are unusual shoes," she said. "Are they for hiking?"

"Not exactly. They're high-grip climbing shoes for spelunking — exploring caves," Andy explained.

"Sounds like a dangerous hobby," said Dr. Emily. "But I suppose it's nothing for someone who handles venomous snakes."

"Give me the snakes any day," said Tracy, winking at Mandy.

"Actually, most spelunkers are very cautious," Andy said. "Just this morning, we pulled out of an exercise in Lulworth because the sea was too rough. We went to the Gray Horse for coffee instead."

"That's even more risky," Mandy joked, and although she knew the truth behind the ghostly sightings, she couldn't resist adding, "You might have bumped into Harry Hawkins!"

Mandy might have been able to joke about the legendary ghost, but the chance that there were modern-day smugglers in the area was no joking matter. For the rest of that day, she kept worrying about Paige and Fabian. If the smugglers were like Harry Hawkins and his counterparts of old, they would use the coves and cliffs to bring in their cargo. And they'd probably work under the cover of darkness, when Paige and Fabian were on the cliff-tops, too. Mandy shuddered to think what might happen if Paige came across them. People who could happily deal in endangered animals would be ruthless about keeping their illegal trade a secret. Mandy had to warn Paige — and fast.

But getting ahold of her proved impossible. Mandy looked in the telephone directory, but there was no Cleary listed in West Chaldon. She'd have gone to Paige's home, except she didn't know the address. She was tempted to ask her mom and dad for help, but she'd promised to say nothing to anyone yet. *But Paige and Fabian are in real danger. I've got to do something.*

Her only option was to wait for Paige in Spooky Hollow.

That night, after her parents had gone to bed, Mandy crept out of the house. She left Pala sleeping in her basket in the living room. It was a clear, starry night so she wouldn't need the services of her personal tracker dog. When she arrived at the grove, she looked around to check that she was alone. Satisfied that she was, she tiptoed to the stable, shining her flashlight on the ground. It was deathly quiet; not even a breath of wind disturbed the autumn leaves still clinging to the branches.

I hope they haven't already gone out, Mandy thought, seeing that the door was ajar. "Paige? Fabian?" she whispered.

A dark, flowing shape loomed up before her then shot past her out of the door. Mandy gave a cry of alarm before she realized it was Paige and Fabian.

"Hey! It's me," Mandy said loudly.

Paige reined in the stallion at the edge of the trees. She was wearing her homemade cloak again. She pushed it back off her face. "You nearly scared us to death, Mandy. You should have warned me you were coming."

"I *did* come to warn you," Mandy said. "About smugglers."

"Oh, sure. Ghost smugglers," Paige said with a cynical laugh.

"No. *Real* smugglers," Mandy said, and told her about the tuatara and Dr. Emily's guess that reptiles were being sneaked into the country on the Dorset coast. "So you can't keep riding Fabian at night."

"I have to," said Paige. "He needs exercise."

"But not here and not at night," Mandy argued.

Fabian was growing restless. He stamped the ground and shook his head. Paige stroked his neck. "It's OK, boy," she said. "We'll go in a minute." She looked down at Mandy. "It's much safer to ride after dark so that if people see us, they'll think we're ghosts."

"Look, Paige," Mandy said, feeling impatient. "Not everyone believes in ghosts. And I bet smugglers wouldn't be too . . ." She broke off abruptly. She'd heard a faint sound, like a voice. "Did you hear that?" she whispered.

"No," said Paige, just as a shout rang out from farther along the hollow.

"Over here!"

Mandy and Paige exchanged a look of horror. "Get Fabian inside!" Mandy said, switching off the flashlight.

Paige slid down from the stallion, landing with a soft thud. She led him into the stable, closed the door, and came back to Mandy. "Do you see anything?" she asked.

Mandy shook her head. She remembered the other night when she, Jay, and Emma had to keep calling out to find each other. "I wonder if someone's lost? Maybe we should go and see in case they need help."

They crept through the trees and down through the gully. They were nearing the brambles when there was another shout, louder than the first. "Watch it, Pete!"

There was a darting movement beyond the brambles.

Mandy glimpsed a bulky human shape moving up the slope to the clifftop. "OK. Let's get the next one," called a man's voice, and Mandy saw another shadowy form appear from the brambles and start up the slope.

"Get down!" she warned Paige. These were not late-night hikers who were lost or in trouble. They were people who knew exactly where they were. And from their furtive behavior, they seemed to be up to no good. Mandy's first instinct was to run back to the shed to hide. But even though the men had disappeared over the top of the slope, they were too close. If they came back now, they'd easily see Mandy and Paige running away. "We've got to hide," she whispered.

They crawled beside the stream, heading for the brambles. Not far from where the men had gone up the bank, Mandy noticed a bush at the top that would provide some cover. Beckoning to Paige to follow her, she crept up the slope, ready to flatten herself on the ground if the men appeared. Nearing the top, she crawled the last few feet to the bush, tucked herself behind it, and peered out in the direction the men had gone.

A shiver ran down her spine. She could see the men quite clearly now. They were on the edge of the cliff, their shapes outlined by the glow from a lantern standing on a rock. They were pulling on ropes and as Mandy watched, two wooden crates appeared over the edge. It looked exactly like some of the scenes on the place mats in the Gray Horse restaurant.

"Careful!" one of the men said when the crates swung into each other. Above the clack of wood against wood came the thrum of a boat engine from below the cliff. "We don't want any more dead ones," the man added.

Two things jolted Mandy. The first was the man's voice. It sounded familiar, so familiar that Mandy placed it almost at once. *He's the hiker!*

The second thing was what he'd said: *We don't want any more dead ones.*

These men had to be the smugglers! *And we've caught them in the act,* Mandy thought. Those crates were bound to contain more reptiles — not necessarily alive after their long, cruel journey.

"We have to get help," she whispered to Paige who was crouching just behind her. She tried to get a good look at the men so she could identify them later, and was just about to duck out from behind the bush when Paige stood up and slipped on the damp grass. "Oh!" Mandy gasped as Paige tumbled head over heels down the slope and landed in the stream with a splash and a cry of pain.

Along the cliff, the men spun around. "What was that?" said one, looking straight toward the bush.

Mandy froze, her heart thudding like a bass drum. Was she about to be discovered by modern-day smugglers?

Ten

A sharp twig stabbed Mandy's cheek but she didn't dare to move her face. The man she'd met before was coming straight toward her, the beam from his flashlight was sweeping back and forth across the bush and down the slope to the stream.

Don't move, Paige, Mandy willed her silently.

The man was just yards away now. "Who's there?" he demanded, the beam shining right into her eyes.

The game's up, Mandy thought, blinking into the bright light. Should she stand up and go toward him, pretending she'd lost her dog again? Pretending she hadn't noticed the crates and that she wasn't even remotely curious as to what the men were doing out on the cliffs at night? Preparing to step out from the bush, Mandy opened her mouth to say, "Only me," when the beam swung away from her and darkness shielded her once more.

The shaft of light cut across the slope, skimming over the bracken and picking out the silvery thread of the stream. Any moment now and it would find Paige.

"There you are," said the man, holding the flashlight steady. "Come out."

Mandy's heart plunged. Across the other side of the gully, a figure was scampering up the slope, the beam tracing its progress.

Mandy's heart soared. It was a fox!

The man laughed. "Just a fox," he said. Shaking his head, he jogged back to his accomplice.

Mandy slipped out from behind the bush and stole down to the gully. Daring to switch on her flashlight, she found Paige crawling out of the stream.

"Are you OK?" Mandy asked, holding out her hand to help her up.

Paige grabbed her hand. "I think so. My foot hurts a little, that's all. Are the men gone?"

"They're still on the cliff," Mandy said in a whisper. "We've got to get out of here before they come back."

Paige started to pull herself up, but when she tried to put weight on her injured foot, she collapsed to the ground. "My ankle!" she groaned.

Mandy bent down and put her arm around Paige's waist. "Hold on to me and I'll pull you up," she said. "I'll help you back to the shed, then I'll get my mom and dad."

But even leaning heavily on Mandy, Paige couldn't move. "It really hurts," she said.

"Can you hop?" Mandy said. "I'll support you."

Paige looked over to where the trees formed a dark mass that hid the stable from view. "I'll never make it. You go." She gently eased herself into a clump of ferns with her legs stretched out to one side. "I'll wait here."

"It's too dangerous," Mandy said. "And it'll be a while before I get back."

"Not if you take Fabian," said Paige, sucking in her breath as she eased off her shoe.

Mandy knew she had no choice. No one knew where they'd gone, so it could be hours — all night even — before anyone noticed they were missing.

"Fabian's fast," Paige told her. "You'll be home in no time."

"What if the smugglers see you?" Mandy said.

"They won't." Paige sounded confident, but Mandy knew she was putting on a brave face. To be alone in

Spooky Hollow, cold, wet, hurt, and barely out of sight of dangerous smugglers needed nerves of steel. "I could hide under these ferns," Paige added.

It didn't seem much, but it was the only choice. Mandy helped Paige remove her damp jacket. Then she took off her own coat and tucked it around her. She gave Paige the flashlight and started dragging large ferns over her. Within a few minutes, big green fronds covered her completely. A person would have to walk over them to know that someone was hiding there. The camouflage made it easier for Mandy to leave Paige. "I promise I won't be long," she said.

"Just be careful," came Paige's muffled reply from under the pile of greenery. "Fabian rides like the wind when you give him his head."

"That's exactly what we need," Mandy said.

Fabian snorted when Mandy opened the stable door. He peered out into the dark, as if he was looking for Paige. Mandy stroked his shoulder while she checked the length of the stirrups. "Paige is hurt," she told him. "We've got to get help." She led him out into the night, glad he was already saddled up.

They moved silently through the trees, pausing at the edge. Across the other side of Spooky Hollow, the smugglers were just visible on the clifftop.

"It's now or never!" Mandy said when it looked as if

the men were concentrating on pulling up another crate from the bottom of the cliff. She vaulted onto Fabian's back and picked up the reins. "Go, Fabian!"

The stallion sprang straight into a gallop, and Mandy had to grab onto his mane to keep herself in the saddle. Adjusting his stride so smoothly Mandy only just felt it, Fabian cleared the stream with a smooth, faultless jump, then powered his way around the brambles and up the slope. In the dark, no landmarks stood out, not even the path Mandy had followed so many times. She was going to have to rely on her sense of direction to get them back to the clinic.

They charged on, into the icy wind that cut through Mandy's sweater, but all she could think of was Paige lying hurt and vulnerable in Spooky Hollow. She leaned forward in the saddle, like a jockey racing to the finishing post. Fabian raced across the Down, his hooves thudding in time with the rhythmic rasping of his breath. If the situation hadn't been so desperate, it would have been one of the most thrilling rides of Mandy's life.

Sooner than seemed possible, a welcome light appeared in the distance, twinkling like a firefly. With each stride that Fabian took, the glow grew bigger and brighter and was soon joined by others. Roofs and chimneys appeared, and Mandy recognized the thatched roof of the clinic. Before long, the back fence became

visible. At the speed Fabian was going, it seemed to be rushing toward them. "Whoa, Fabian!" she said, tugging the reins.

But Fabian had other ideas. Like a champion show-jumper, he soared over the fence, landing smoothly on the lawn and slithering to a stop at the back door. At once, Pala started barking and a window was flung open upstairs. Mandy looked up into the face of a very startled-looking Dr. Adam.

"What's going on?"

"Call the police, quickly!" Mandy said.

"Whose horse is that?" said her dad, staring with a shocked expression at the stallion.

"Later, Dad," Mandy said, quickly dismounting. "Get the police. Please. It's urgent."

Dr. Emily appeared in the window next to Mandy's dad. "Mandy Hope! What are you doing riding at this time of the night?"

"Paige is hurt and we've found the reptile smugglers," Mandy blurted out. "We've got to get back to the cliff before they leave. And before Paige gets hypothermia!"

"She's out there on her own?" Dr. Emily looked furious. "What were you two doing out there in the dark?"

"I'll explain everything later," Mandy said. "Please, just get dressed. Fast!" She led Fabian to an empty store-room. There was a plastic bowl in one corner and she filled it with water. "I'll get you some real food later," Mandy promised, hugging him before she went out. She paused at the door. "You were amazing, Fabian. Thank you."

He gave her a penetrating look and snorted as if urging her to hurry back to Paige.

Within five minutes, two police vehicles sped through the gates. One was a car and the other, a van full of officers. After hearing Mandy's story, the officer in charge, Inspector Cuff, ordered the van to follow his car. Then he radioed the station and asked for a police boat to be sent to the foot of the cliff. He asked Mandy and her parents to go with him, so that Mandy could pinpoint exactly where the smugglers were.

They drove through a farm gate onto the Down and bumped across the uneven ground. After a few minutes, still some way from the hollow, the detective radioed the van and told the officers to go the rest of the way on foot. Mandy and her mom and dad got out, too. Fanning out, and with Mandy in the middle next to Inspector Cuff, they moved silently toward Spooky Hollow.

"Where exactly where they?" the inspector asked Mandy.

"On the cliff edge," she replied. "But it looked like they were dragging the crates down the slope."

"Then we'll approach the hollow in an arc so no one

can get away," the officer decided. At the edge of the hollow, he signaled to the Hopes to stay behind a bush while he ordered his men to head down to the gully.

"Be careful, Paige is hiding under some ferns next to the stream," Mandy reminded him.

"We'll make sure she's safe," Inspector Cuff promised.

Minutes ticked by and nothing happened. All around, it was deathly quiet. So quiet, Mandy could hear her own heart beating and her mom and dad breathing next to her. She felt herself growing tense. Something was wrong. What if the smugglers had found Paige and were using her as a hostage? Or they'd bundled her down the cliff to the boat and were already halfway across the Channel to France?

But just as she pictured a motor boat speeding away with a terrified Paige, a commotion broke out from somewhere in Spooky Hollow. There were loud shouts and thudding sounds, like people were racing up the slope.

Mandy peered out from behind the bush.

"Move it, Brad!" she heard a man shout, and a moment later she saw a figure come over the edge of the hollow only yards from where she and her parents were hiding. Seconds behind him came another man and as he started to sprint after the first, he slipped and fell to the ground. "Hold up, Peter!" he yelled, and Mandy recognized the voice of the hiker again.

But where were the police? Had the smugglers given them the slip? Mandy bit her lip, watching anxiously as Brad picked himself up and raced after Pete. "They're going to get away," she whispered to her parents. "We'll have to go after them."

"No," said her dad, grabbing her arm. "The police know what they're doing."

With that, the Down was suddenly bathed in light, as if someone had switched on a powerful spotlight and trained it on the two men. They stopped and looked around in confusion, then spun around as an engine started up and the source of the light was revealed. It was one of the police vans, and it was heading straight for the smugglers.

The men charged back the way they'd come, only to find themselves engulfed by a wave of policemen who surged over the edge of Spooky Hollow.

There were sounds of scuffling and a raised voice or two, then Mandy heard someone say, "Get them to the station," and she watched with relief as the policemen frogmarched the smugglers to the waiting van.

"Phew!" breathed Dr. Emily at Mandy's side. "That was intense."

"Pretty good work, too," said Dr. Adam. "Now for Paige . . ."

But Mandy was already sprinting down the slope toward the spot where she'd left her friend. With a sigh of relief, she found Paige — already sitting up, and pushing away the ferns. "Are you OK?" she gasped.

"That'll teach them a lesson!" said Paige.

"The police catching them?" Mandy asked.

"That, but I gave them the fright of their lives, too!" said Paige. "They shouted something about a police boat, and the next minute they were running down from the cliff toward me."

"You must have been terrified," Mandy said.

"Only that they'd get away," Paige said just as Mandy's parents arrived, looking shocked to see her sitting among the heap of ferns. "So, when they got really close, I wailed like a banshee. You should have seen the looks on their faces." Paige chuckled. "They were so scared, they charged back straight through the stream and up the slope."

"And straight into the arms of the police!" Mandy laughed. "Serves them right."

"Well, we don't know that yet," said Dr. Adam. "The police will have to see if there's any evidence to convict them. There could be anything in those boxes," said Dr. Adam. He knelt down to look at Paige's ankle.

"Looks like a sprain. We'll get you home and strap it up for you."

"You're very lucky it's nothing worse," said Dr. Emily. She folded her arms and looked angrily at Mandy and Paige. "You could have got yourselves into a lot of trouble. Not to mention what would have happened if those men had seen you! Does your mom know you're out here, Paige?"

Paige looked down and shook her head. "She's probably still at work."

"Well, as soon as we get back to the house, you're going to call her," said Mandy's mom. "In the meantime, I want the full story. You've really crossed the line this time, Mandy."

Mandy cleared her throat. "Well . . ." she began, and looked up the cliff where policemen were shining powerful flashlights around.

"There are dozens of crates here!" she heard one shout, and then, moments later, "Take a look at this. It looks like a dragon!"

"Wow!" called out the same police officer. "Is it dead?"

Mandy went cold. "Not another one!" she said. "We've got to help!" The explanation her mom wanted would have to wait. She ran up to the cliff, glancing back to see her dad giving Paige a piggyback up the slope.

When Mandy saw how many reptiles were squashed

up inside the crates, and how miserable and lethargic they were, she was furious. There were all sorts of species — many, like Spike and the tuatara, that Mandy had never seen or heard of before. Her dad identified a horned lizard from America, a girdle lizard from South Africa, and two Nile monitor lizards. There were even a few tortoises, some from America and others from Africa.

Mandy felt sick about what the poor animals must have gone through on the long journey from their homes. But it was the sight of two Komodo dragons that had died that upset her the most. *How many more will there be*? she wondered, dreading what the unopened crates would reveal.

Working as fast as they could, they began transferring the boxes to the second police van. Paige couldn't help move the crates, but she sat on a rock, wrapped in a big jacket a policeman had loaned her and held up a bright searchlight.

Inspector Cuff called Tracy on his mobile to warn her they would be bringing the reptiles straight to the center. "She promised to go there right away to prepare for them," he said when he hung up. "She's asked us to question the men and find out exactly how many reptiles they brought in recently, and what happened to them. They've already admitted to having lost two lizards a few days ago. A panel in one of the crates split open but they only noticed it after they'd delivered it to their contact twenty miles from here."

"Spike and the Tuatara!" Mandy exclaimed, understanding now how they'd ended up where they'd been found. After he'd escaped, Spike must have had enough strength to find his way to Jay and Emma's garden. The poor Tuatara wasn't so lucky. Like so many of the others, he must have already been weak when he slipped out of the crate. His final desperate journey in search of freedom was just too much for him, and he'd died before a caring person could rescue him.

Determined that not one more reptile would be lost, Mandy worked even faster than before to help get the crates into the police van. At last, half an hour later, the work was done and the precious creatures were on their way to the rescue center. But the night wasn't over yet.

Despite the smugglers having been foiled, Dr. Emily was still furious. "You're not off the hook. What do you have to say for yourselves?"

"And don't leave out a single detail," said Dr. Adam. He hoisted Paige onto his back and they headed back to the police car.

"Well . . ." Mandy hesitated. She knew she was in serious trouble and that holding things back would make it worse. But spilling the beans meant that Paige was going to be in big trouble, too. "It's about Fabian," she said, desperately trying to keep from complicating things for her new friend. "He's — "

Paige interrupted her. "It's OK, Mandy. I know I can't keep this a secret anymore." She told Mandy's parents about Abraham's death, how he'd made her promise to look after Fabian, how she'd taken him to the shed so he wouldn't be auctioned off to strangers, and how Mandy had found them a few nights earlier. "If it hadn't been for Mandy, Fabian might have fallen over the cliff! She also noticed he had a cut on his fetlock and told me what to do about it," Paige finished.

"That's great," said Dr. Emily, her face still hard. "But what exactly were you doing out there that night, Mandy? We told you not to go onto the Down after dark."

"I know," Mandy said, feeling very uncomfortable. "It's just that I *had* to find out who the horse and rider were."

Dr. Emily was not impressed. "Your dad and I do not approve of you sneaking behind our backs. Beginning next week, you're grounded for four weekends."

"But . . ." Mandy began, but then thought better about trying to protest when her mom shot her the angriest glare yet.

Later, back at the cottage, with her ankle neatly strapped, Paige called her mom. Mrs. Cleary was as shocked as Mandy's parents to hear that Paige had been riding near the top of the cliff at night. She was also furious that Paige had taken Fabian from the farm.

"She said I had no right to interfere," Paige reported after she'd finished talking to her mom. "She's coming to get me, and in the morning I've got to get someone to help me take Fabian back to the farm."

"I'll help you," Mandy promised. They were in Mandy's bedroom, waiting for Mrs. Cleary to arrive.

"It looks like I've lost Fabian after all," Paige said, tears streaming down her cheeks.

Mandy fought to hold back her own tears. "It's not fair. If only we could have found a place for him." She slammed her fist into her pillow in frustration.

"Let's go and see Fabian before my mom gets here," said Paige. "In case he thinks he's been abandoned again."

"OK. He deserves a good feed," said Mandy.

With Paige swinging herself along on a pair of crutches Dr. Adam had found in the utility room, the two friends went out to the shed. But even before they got there, Mandy realized that something was wrong.

"The door's open!" she cried. In a few giant strides she reached the wooden hut. She looked inside. "Fabian's gone!"

Eleven

"I definitely bolted the door," Mandy said. "Someone must have let him out."

"No," said Paige, "he got out by himself. He used to undo the bolt on his stable with his teeth until Abraham put in an extra one that was out of his reach."

"Smart horse," Mandy said.

"Not *that* smart," said Paige, "or he'd have stayed here where he was safe. He could be anywhere now." Her face crumpled.

"He might not have gone too far," Mandy said. An idea came to her, one that seemed entirely possible. "Maybe he's gone back to Spooky Hollow to look for you."

"You think so?" said Paige.

Mandy was warming to the idea; after all, she'd seen the extraordinary bond between Paige and Fabian. "Yes."

"Would your dad drive us back there?" Paige asked as they returned to the house.

"I'm not sure," said Mandy. "He and Mom are furious."

They'd just gone in when Paige's mom pulled up outside. They waited for her in the hall, trading nervous glances as she walked up the path, her expression grim.

Paige whispered to Mandy, "She's mad, too."

Mandy jumped as the phone on the hall table rang. She picked it up, glad to have something to do. "Mandy Hope speaking," she said.

"Could I speak to one of the vets, please?" asked the woman on the line. Just then, Mrs. Cleary came through the door.

"Can I tell them who's calling?" Mandy asked. "Is it an emergency?" The clock on the wall showed it was nearly eleven o'clock. People didn't usually call the vet this late unless it was something very serious.

Mrs. Cleary was signaling to Paige to go to the car. Paige bit her lip and looked at Mandy, then back at her mom. Mandy knew she desperately wanted to find Fabian.

"It's not a true emergency, I suppose," said the caller,

who sounded oddly familiar. "It's just that I was woken up by a loose horse clattering around in my yard."

Mandy's heart skipped a beat. "A horse?"

Paige was about to go through the door but she spun around, her eyes wide.

"An Arabian stallion," said the caller. "I was wondering if anyone has reported him missing."

"They sure have!" Mandy said, and she thought she'd burst with relief. "Where can we come to see if he's the same one?" She was convinced it was Fabian but she had to see for herself.

"Middle Farm, just past West Chaldon. My name's Jemima Broadbridge."

Mandy could hardly believe her ears. "We know exactly where you are," she said. "Paige and I were there just yesterday. We'll see if we can come over right away."

Mrs. Cleary's expression softened a little when she heard about Fabian breaking out and how desperately worried Mandy and Paige were. "At least you know he's safe," she said. "Now, wait in the car for me, Paige, while I go up and have a word with Mandy's parents."

"After that, can we go to Middle Farm? Please, Mom?" Paige begged. "Just to make sure it is Fabian."

Mrs. Cleary stopped at the bottom of the stairs. It seemed like ages before she turned around. "The two of you have sure pushed your luck tonight, haven't you?" She sighed. "But I suppose another half hour won't hurt."

Upstairs, a door opened and Dr. Adam called down, "Mandy, is that Mrs. Cleary?"

"Yes, Dad," she said, and she heard the sound of footsteps coming down the stairs.

Mrs. Cleary came over to stand in front of Paige. "I know that horse means everything to you. Just like you mean to me. That's why I was so upset when I heard what you were up to tonight." She put her arms around Paige and hugged her. "Of course we'll go and check if it's Fabian. I only wish I could afford to let you keep him."

Mandy's parents were amazed to hear where Fabian had ended up. "Mom and I will drive you over," Dr. Adam said to Mandy. "But I don't want any more tricks from you tonight."

When they all arrived at Middle Farm, Jemima was waiting for them outside the small stable block. "I've put him in here for now," she said, leading them inside.

Fabian didn't seem at all upset after his second cross-country adventure in the dark. He looked out of his stall, his small ears pricked. When he saw Paige and Mandy, he whinnied.

"What are you doing here, Fabian?" said Paige, putting her arms around him.

"Maybe he's checking to see if the stable's any good," said Jemima. She smiled at Paige and Mandy. "Have you two had any more thoughts about stabling him here?"

"Well, the thing is . . ." Mandy began just as Mrs. Cleary stepped forward. Putting a hand on Paige's shoulder, she said, "What's this about stabling?"

Paige gulped. "We were trying to find somewhere better than Spooky Hollow for him."

"Spooky Hollow!" Jemima looked surprised. "Is that where you've been keeping him?"

Mandy and Paige nodded.

"It's unbelievable, isn't it?" said Dr. Emily and she outlined the rest of the story.

Jemima blinked in amazement. "That *is* an extraordinary tale." She looked at Mandy and Paige. "I'd never have guessed yesterday that you two were up to anything like that. Still, it must have taken a lot of courage, especially when you ran into the smugglers. You really shouldn't have gone behind your parents' backs, but at least everything turned out well." She patted Fabian's shoulder. "And this gorgeous stallion has found a new home!"

"I don't think so," said Mrs. Cleary. "Fabian will have to go back where he came from."

"No, Mom!" Paige burst out, "He'll be sold to someone who doesn't love him like I do!" With that she threw her arms around the stallion again as if she was trying to protect him.

"Look, Paige . . ." began her mom.

But Paige seemed too upset to listen to her. "Abraham said I had to take care of him," she sobbed, burying her face in Fabian's mane.

Mandy saw Fabian turn his head and blow softly into Paige's ear as if he was whispering to her. They seemed closer than ever. It was so wrong that they would have to be separated.

Mrs. Cleary went to stand next to Paige. She put her arm across her shoulder. "I know that's what he told you, and I really wish you could keep that promise."

"I *can* keep it," Paige said earnestly. "I know what Fabian needs and how to take care of him."

"Perhaps," said her mom. "But there's a lot more to it than just riding him."

"Paige wasn't only riding him," Mandy added, as desperate as Paige that Fabian should stay with her. "She was doing her best for him under very hard conditions."

"We all realize that," said Dr. Emily. "But as Paige's mom said, it's a big responsibility to own a horse."

"A vet, a farrier, daily grooming, proper feed . . . there's all that to consider," said Dr. Adam. "And of course, Fabian's a stallion and they need expert handling. . . ."

"I know all that and I *am* responsible," Paige insisted, looking around at Mrs. Cleary.

Her mom smiled at her. "I guess, in a rather backward fashion, you've shown me that. I would have preferred it, though, if you'd told me about your plan instead of smuggling Fabian to Spooky Hollow and sneaking off there after dark."

"I'm really sorry, Mom," said Paige. "I just didn't know what else to do. Fabian can't be sold off like a piece of farm machinery."

Mrs. Cleary sighed. "Look, honey," she said, "there's something I haven't told you."

"What?" asked Paige, the color draining from her face as if she expected really bad news.

Mandy held her breath, half-expecting to hear that Fabian had already been sold.

"I got a call last week from the lawyer handling Abraham's estate," continued Mrs. Cleary. "In his will, Abraham did stipulate what will happen to Fabian. He's not going to be sold with the farm." Her mom paused, and the suspense was killing Mandy. Paige's eyes welled up with tears, anticipating the worst. "He wanted you to have him, Paige."

"Oh!" cried Paige at the same time that Mandy slapped her hand to her mouth in surprise.

"But I'm afraid the reason I haven't said anything to you until now, Paige, is because I don't see any way this can work."

"What?" Paige demanded, pulling away from Fabian, a wave of new disappointment covering her face.

Mandy turned around to see Paige's mom shaking her head. "I know this horse means everything to you, Paige. But we simply can't afford him. The livery fees alone are completely unaffordable."

Paige looked devastated. "I'll get a paper route," she said desperately.

"Actually, I might be able to help out," said Jemima.

"What do you mean?" asked Paige.

"Stabling is only going to be a part of my business," Jemima explained. "I want to offer trail rides, too. Fabian would make a fabulous trail horse."

Mandy and Paige looked at each other uneasily.

"Of course, he wouldn't be mine," Jemima went on as if she'd guessed what was going through Mandy's mind. "I would only use him part-time. That way he'd earn half of his stable fee. To pay for the other half, you could help around the yard, Paige." She looked at Mrs. Cleary. "So he wouldn't cost you a penny."

There was silence as everyone waited for Mrs. Cleary to answer. Paige looked at her mom with pleading eyes while standing close to Fabian, one arm around his neck again.

Eventually, Mrs. Cleary spoke. "There will be conditions, Paige. No more sneaking out behind my back. No hare-brained schemes that could put you in danger, and no attempts to get out of your responsibilities to Fabian. And doing your share of the work means just that — every day, come rain or shine, school days, holidays, Christmas . . ."

"I swear!" said Paige, her eyes shining. "You'll see, Mom. I won't let you — or Fabian — down!"

"Then I suppose you've got yourself a horse at last, sweetheart," said Mrs. Cleary and she patted Fabian's neck. "Welcome to the family, gorgeous boy!"

It was such incredible news that Paige seemed to forget all about her sprained ankle. She whirled around to hug her mom, dropping her crutches and losing her balance. Dr. Adam put out his arm to steady her, but not before Fabian stretched his neck forward to offer his own form of support.

"You were right about him," said Dr. Adam to Paige, who was holding on to his mane. "He's a very sensitive horse."

"And smart," Mandy said. "Smart enough to find a

new owner and a new home and help crack a reptile-smuggling ring all in one night!"

Two days later, on Halloween, Mandy and Paige met at Middle Farm. They were going onto Chaldon Down for the last time before Mandy went home the next day. But this time they were going in daylight. Paige still couldn't walk properly, so she rode Fabian while Mandy jogged beside them with Pala on a leash. They were heading for Spooky Hollow, to get the grooming kit and antiseptic powder they had left there. It wasn't long before Pala picked up the scent of a rabbit and started tugging on the leash. When they were just yards from Spooky Hollow, Pala finally managed to slip out of her collar.

"Oh, well," Mandy said as Pala ran toward the dip and disappeared over the edge. "At least we know it isn't dangerous for her down there now."

Paige smiled. "No ghosts and no smugglers."

They reached the edge of Spooky Hollow in time for Mandy to see Pala vanish among the brambles at the bottom. "Wait here," she said to Paige. "I'll go get her." She ran down the slope, calling Pala's name. Pala didn't respond so Mandy decided to go in after her, in case she'd gotten stuck.

It was dank and dark under the tangled branches, and very eerie. The trickling of the stream was the only sound, and there wasn't a trace of Pala, not even a paw print. *How could she just disappear?* Mandy wondered.

At that moment, the ground gave way beneath her. "Help!" she cried, landing heavily on her side.

She found herself underground, in a rock-lined tunnel. A yard or two above her, daylight flooded in where the ground had collapsed. "Just my luck to find a booby trap," she said. She moved her legs and arms and was glad that nothing felt broken or sprained or even bruised. "Third time's the charm, at least," she said. She stood up to haul herself out of the tunnel but when she turned around, she stopped dead.

In front of her were dozens of wooden boxes. They were stacked three high against the rocky wall, and in some places stood two or three deep.

"Not more reptiles!" Mandy gasped in dismay. "Please let the poor creatures be OK!" she begged as she started to pry open a lid. She shut her eyes, convinced she'd open them to the heartbreaking sight of dead or dying reptiles.

She felt the lid come away from the box. Reluctantly, she opened her eyes. Mandy gasped as she reached inside. It was not a scaly creature, but the softest material imaginable. "Silk!" she cried, holding up a length of gossamer, ivory-colored fabric. She pulled out another piece, and another, wrapping them around her neck like scarves. Excited, she tore the lid off another box. This one was full of lace, intricately woven with flower patterns. She flung open more boxes to reveal even more silk, more lace, and tea leaves, too — loose and surprisingly aromatic. "Buried treasure!"

She took a handful of tea and let it fall through her fingers to the ground. She remembered what the owner of the Gray Horse restaurant had told her about the rumors. "Harry Hawkins's last stash!" As the tea sifted through her fingers, she could have sworn she heard a

voice from down the ages: *"Ye'll find the crop in the secret chamber under the ground."*

Another voice, this one more immediate, was calling to her then. "Where are you, Mandy?" It was Paige.

"In Harry's secret chamber!" Mandy called, and with the silk wrapped around her neck and her pockets bulging with lace, she climbed out of the tunnel and made her way back through the brambles.

She emerged to find the others waiting for her in the dip: Pala, wagging her tail with innocent delight, Paige sitting in the saddle looking perplexed, and the gorgeous stallion standing regally as if he were the lord of Spooky Hollow.

"I just met my first *real* Halloween ghost!" Mandy laughed. She held up a piece of lace. It might not be the sort of gold or silver treasure people dreamed about, but it was a precious piece of Dorset history, one that was nearly four hundred years old. Paige and Fabian's ghostly antics had been protecting the traditional smugglers after all. "Harry Hawkins's last crop. It was here all along, at the bottom of Spooky Hollow!"

ABOUT THE AUTHOR

Ben M. Baglio was born in New York and grew up in a small town in southern New Jersey. He was the only boy in a family with three sisters.

Ben spent a lot of his childhood reading. English was always his favorite subject, and after graduating from high school, he went on to study English Literature at the University of Pennsylvania. During his coursework, he was able to spend a year in Edinburgh, Scotland.

After graduation, Ben worked as a children's book editor in New York City. He also wrote his first book, which was about the Olympics in ancient Greece. Five years later, he took a job at a publishing house in England.

Ben is the author of the Dolphin Diaries series, and is perhaps most well-known for the Animal Ark and Animal Ark Hauntings series. These books were originally published in England (under the pseudonym Lucy Daniels) and have since gone on to be published in the U. S. and translated into fifteen languages.

Aside from writing, Ben enjoys scuba diving and swimming, music, and movies. He has a beagle named Bob, who is by his side whenever he writes.

THERE'S ALWAYS AN ADVENTURE AT
BIG APPLE BARN!

BIG APPLE BARN
HAPPY GO LUCKY

BIG APPLE BARN
HAPPY'S BIG PLAN

BIG APPLE BARN
A SASSY SURPRISE

BIG APPLE BARN
SADDLE UP, HAPPY!

by KRISTIN EARHART
Illustrations by JOHN STEVEN GURNEY
SCHOLASTIC

by KRISTIN EARHART
Illustrations by JOHN STEVEN GURNEY
SCHOLASTIC

When Happy Go Lucky, a young quarter pony,
is moved from his home to the stables at Big Apple Barn,
there's no telling what will happen.

SCHOLASTIC
www.scholastic.com

READ THEM ALL!

SCHOLASTIC and associated logos are trademarks
and/or registered trademarks of Scholastic Inc.

BABB